THE TIME TRAP

By
HENRY KUTTNER

W0008659

ARMCHAIR FICTION
PO Box 4369, Medford, Oregon   97501-0168

*For more information about Armchair Books and products, visit our
website at…*

www.armchairfiction.com

Or email us at…

armchairfiction@yahoo.com

CHAPTER ONE
The Green Monoliths

Kent Mason stumbled to the top of the ridge, staring about him with sun-swollen eyes. His cracked lips twisted wryly as he viewed the endless wilderness of rock, the death-trap of the Arabian desert, dimmed now by driving gusts of icy rain. In the valley below him two pinnacles of rock towered, and as Mason stared at them a curious expression crept over his sunburned face. He recognized those great obelisks, and, recognizing them, knew that his search and his life would end almost simultaneously. For before him lay the fabulous twin towers of the lost city of Al Bekr, ancient metropolis of lost wisdom, City of Science!

Two months ago an expedition had set out from the port of Merbat to search for Al Bekr, and for two months had been vainly pushing through the arid wastes that the Arabs call the Rubh el Khali. Old Doctor Cordell, the leader of the expedition, had pinned his hopes on legends, obscure hints on archaic shards—but mostly upon a tablet that had been recently uncovered on the site of primeval Ur, the import of which was that a remarkable state of civilization had been attained in the "Forbidden City."

According to the inscription, Al Bekr had been merely a little-visited town in the Great Desert, until suddenly, inexplicably, fantastically advanced arts and sciences began to flourish there. But this perfection of science died almost as swiftly as it had been born, for a reason that was either not known or not set down; and the great days of Al Bekr were over forever. It was, in fact, a compressed version of the

Mason and lovely Alasa fought
madly against Greddar Klon's
insensate slaves

Atlantean legend—an advanced, scientific culture destroyed
by some mysterious doom.

Mason, the archeologist of the party, was also the
youngest in age. Now, through the irony of fate, he had
accomplished, unguided and lost, what his colleagues had
despaired of doing. Doctor Cordell had decided to give up
the search and return to Merbat, and when Mason,
determined to investigate a little-known mountain range
nearby, had insisted on one last try, Cordell had refused to
permit it.

That morning Mason slipped away from camp, taking a
speedy camel, thinking he could reach the mountains and
rejoin the slow-traveling party in a day or two at the most.
But his plans had miscarried. The camel had fallen, breaking

THE TIME TRAP

by HENRY KUTTNER

Author of "Avengers of Space," etc.

STARTLING BOOK-LENGTH NOVEL OF MEN AND WOMEN DRAWN FROM TIME-SECTORS FIVE HUNDRED CENTURIES APART AND HURLED INTO CIVILIZATION'S DAWN-ERA!

its leg. The compass had been smashed, and for three days Mason had been lost in this desolate, sun-baked inferno. The water had not lasted long. He had shot a vulture and forced himself to eat the tough, stringy meat; then, during his nearly delirious wanderings, Mason had lost his revolver. Now, hollow-eyed and exhausted, he saw beneath him Al Bekr, City of Science!

The centuries had left little of the fabled metropolis. Two giant pinnacles protruding from the drifted sand, a riven block half buried here and there. That was all. Grim and desolate in the drenching rain, the valley lay lifeless and silent below. Yet there would be shelter there, and the storm was momentarily growing fiercer. There are few storms in the Rubh el Khali, but they are cataclysmic in their fury. Lightning forked above Mason.

He made his way down the slope, staggering in his weakness. The tumbled fragments of masonry seemed to increase in size as he drew nearer. The city in its heyday must have been an awe-inspiring sight.

Thunder snarled behind the hills. The two obelisks were not far apart, and provided some shelter. Mason collapsed against one of them. He breathed a great sigh of relief, let his aching muscles relax. Then, suddenly, his lean face was alight with interest. The surface of the monolith against which he leaned was not stone. Rough, worn, pitted with the teeth of the ages, it was nevertheless unmistakably metal!

But what race of people could have reared these tremendous spires, nearly forty feet high? It was impossible. Mason examined the texture of the metal, frowning. He did not recognize it. Hard and rough-grained, with a peculiar greenish tinge, it was apparently some unfamiliar alloy.

Ominously thunder growled overhead. Then without warning. lightning struck. Like an incandescent white-hot sword it raced down the skies, enveloping the twin spires in blinding brilliance. Mason felt himself lifted, flung aside. He had a momentary glimpse of a sheet of roaring, flashing flame playing between the two pinnacles. There was a moment of unendurable tension, as though the air was becoming surcharged with electricity. Then there was wrenching agony that tore at the fiber of Mason's being, agony such that he shrieked aloud and knew that no sound came from his paralyzed lips. He felt a surge of incredibly swift movement. Blackness took him, blackness, and vertigo, and then quickly the shadow fled back and vanished. Blazing light flared into his eyes.

The desolate valley of Al Bekr—was gone! Gone the drenching rain, the growling of thunder overhead, the wet sand beneath his body! He lay on his back, staring up with amazed eyes at a tremendously high roof, lit with strange green brilliance. And towering up toward that high-arched ceiling were—the monoliths!

The twin towers—but changed! Gone were the scars and pits of centuries of erosion. Their surfaces were smooth, glistening with greenish sheen, and beyond them marched row upon row of fantastic machines, shining and brilliant in the strange light. Mason had never seen such machinery and could only guess at the purposes of oddly shaped pistons, wheels, and tubes. The room was wide, circular, paved and walled with white stone. In the walls at intervals were set bars of some greenish substance that glowed with cold flame.

Mason put out a hand, touched the smooth surface of the green monolith beside him. The touch was reassuring. He wasn't mad, he told himself desperately. The lightning stroke must have unleashed some undreamed-of power in the mysterious towers, wrought some astounding change, which as yet he could not understand. He got slowly to his feet, half expecting the incredible scene to shift and change to the rain-drenched desert valley.

Behind him a voice barked a deep-toned question.

Mason turned quickly. A man stood near, a swarthy, stock figure in loincloth and sandals; startlingly pale blue eyes set in a harsh, weather-beaten face of seamed tan leather glared at him. A great beak of a nose jutted over the thin-lipped mouth. Again the man snarled his question.

Madness! For he spoke the ancient, forgotten Semite tongue, the purest form of the root-language of Arabic, not used, save among scholars, for almost four thousand years! Some faint inkling of the truth sent the blood dropping from Mason's head. He braced himself, searched his memory gropingly. He knew the root-language...

"I come—from a distant land," Mason said slowly, tentatively, eyeing the great scimitar the warrior carried.

"None may enter this city," the other responded, ferine eyes gleaming. "The Master permits none to enter Al Bekr. Or to leave!"

Al Bekr! Mason cast a swift glance around. Was time, after all, not the changeless thing science had thought it? Had he been flung back into an incredibly distant past by some strange power in the lightning-riven monoliths? Yet these machines, the very masonry beneath his feet, bespoke not the past but the powers of a distant future.

Mason eyed the warrior, felt a tug of recognition pull at his mind. He said, "Al Bekr is not your home."

The man grunted. "It takes no magic to know that. I am a Sumerian."

Mason's jaw dropped. A Sumerian! That mysterious, archaic people whose civilization had existed in the Euphrates-Tigris valleys long before the Semites had come conquering. The warrior, suddenly suspicious, moved forward, his movements catlike, the gleaming scimitar menacing. Swiftly Mason said, "I mean no harm. By El-lil— I swear it!"

The Sumerian's eyes widened. He stared. "El-lil? You swear by—"

Mason nodded. He knew the reverence in which the Sumerians had held the name of their chief god. "I've no wish to be your enemy," he said. A surge of weakness struck him, the culminations of three days and nights in the terrible Rubh el Khali. Mason felt his muscles relaxing, tried vainly to keep his balance while a veil of blackness rushed up to overwhelm him.

The Sumerian sprang forward and put a great arm about Mason's shoulders, supporting him. The warrior thrust his scimitar back into its scabbard, caught Mason in his arms as though the archeologist were a child, and lifted him.

The Sumerian bellowed an oath. "Now by Baal and all the other milk-and-water gods of the north," he concluded, "I fight no man who swears by El-lil!"

Dimly Mason was conscious of being swung across a brawny shoulder, carried through interminable green-lit corridors. He was too weak to resist. At last he was deposited lightly on a mound of furs. He felt liquid trickling between his lips, clutched at a flask the warrior held and lifted it. Water…no, not water, though the liquor was tasteless and very cold. Energy seemed to trickle through every fiber of Mason's parched body with the fluid. He drained the flask, then put it aside.

His weakness had gone. He sat up, staring about the room—bare, stone-walled, carpeted with furs. The Sumerian put down the flask with a ruefully thirsty glance. "Now who are you?" he growled. "Nobody in this cursed land knows of El-lil. And you are no man of Sumer."

Mason chose his words carefully. "I come from a distant land," he said. "A land far to the west, where El-lil's fame has traveled. How I came here—I don't know."

"The Master would know. How are you named?"

"Mason."

"Ma-zhon." He rolled the syllables upon his tongue, giving them a curiously guttural sound. "And I—well, call me Erech. I was born in the city of Erech, and sometimes it isn't wise for men to give their own names. If I ever leave this city, it would not be well for men to know that I once served Greddar Klon." The Sumerian's harsh face darkened, and he sent a suspicious glance toward Mason. "You know the Master?"

Before Mason could answer a thudding sounded beyond the door. He was startled at the expression that flashed over Erech's face, in which fear and resentment were strangely mingled. The door opened.

Framed in the portal stool—a metal man! Seven feet tall, barrel-bodied, with three jointed legs of silvery metal ending in flat, broad metal plates, the thing stood there—watching! Rubbery, tentacular arms dangled loosely; the head was a metal sphere, incongruously small atop that bulky body, featureless save for a multiple-faceted eye. The robot stared.

The Sumerian did not move. Mason saw the sinews of his right hand crawl beneath the skin. Imperceptibly the hand edged toward the hilt of the scimitar.

The robot spoke, in a flat, toneless voice. "The Master summons you. Come at once."

It turned, retreated. The door shut silently. With a muttered oath Erech relaxed on the furs.

"What—what was that?" Mason asked, feeling a nameless terror stirring within him. The metal creature had seemed alive!

"One of the Master's servants," said the Sumerian, getting to his feet. "One of those he created. Powerful is the Master!" Irony tinged his tone.

"Well, I must go," he went on. "You wait here. I'll be back as soon as I can."

"Didn't that robot see me?" Mason asked uneasily. Erech shrugged.

"El-lil knows! Sometimes they see nothing—sometimes everything. I'll be back soon enough, and we'll find a hiding place for you. There's no time now."

He hurried out, and Mason stared at the closed door, trying to integrate his thoughts. Unconsciously for the last quarter-hour he had been trying to convince himself that this was a dream, a hallucination born of delirium. But he knew this was not so. The reality of this strange city was clear enough, and Mason was young enough to realize how elastic are the boundaries of known science. Time was not fixed, unchangeable. In theory it would be possible to travel into the future or the past. And if in theory—why not in fact?

Strange, yes, and incredible and terrifying—but not impossible. Furtively Mason ran his hand over the smooth surface of the metal wall behind him, smoothed the furs on which he sat. He felt a desperate longing for a cigarette.

There were so many things unexplained! This fantastic city, ruled by a mysterious Master of whom the Sumerian was seemingly terrified. That tied in with the known legends, but it explained woefully little. And it did not tell Mason what he most wanted to know: whether he was among enemies or friends.

A noise in the corridor brought Mason alertly to his feet. Some vague impulse made him open the door, peering out. A robot was advancing along the passage, still almost thirty feet away, and Mason quickly closed the door again, flattening himself against the wall beside it. The creature might pass by, but there was no assurance of that.

The footsteps stopped. The door opened under the pressure of a metallic tentacle. Flattened against the wall Mason saw, from the corner of his eye, the monstrous looming form of the robot moving forward. It had not yet seen him.

The creature crossed the threshold and abruptly halted, as though realizing Mason's proximity. But the man had already sprung forward, thrusting at the robot with his shoulder, attempting to squeeze past into the corridor. He had not realized the frightful power of the thing.

Even caught off balance, the robot was immensely strong. It wheeled, and the arm-tentacles gripped Mason, pulled him back. He tried vainly to fight free.

The creature held him effortlessly, and one coiling limb slid out to close the door. That done, the robot stumped forward into the room, dragging Mason with it, ignoring the man's struggles. The faceted eye glared passionlessly down.

Then Mason caught sight of the empty flask he had drained, that had been flung aside carelessly by the Sumerian. It was lying within easy reach, and with a quick lunge he snatched it up, his fingers tightening about the neck. The robot's eye was not high to reach—and Mason's arm curved in a swift arc, sent the bottle smashing viciously forward.

Glass showered his face painfully. He put all his strength in a frantic attempt to wriggle free, managed to tear the last tentacle from its anchorage about his waist. The robot blundered forward, smashing against the wall. Its eye was shattered, Mason saw; it was blind.

Swiftly he gained the door, crept out quietly into the corridor. Behind him came a thunderous crashing as the robot pounded about the room, reducing it to pulped Wreckage. Mason glanced around. The passage was empty. He could not wait here for Erech; if one robot had been sent, there would be others. Choosing a direction at random, Mason moved cautiously to the left. The corridor was broken at intervals by doors, but he did not try them, fearing to alarm some inhabitant of the city.

But he was given no choice. The distant pounding of feet came mechanically, running toward him, and Mason guessed

14

that additional robots were arriving. A turn in the passage hid them from his sight. He hesitated. Perhaps the ruler of Al Bekr—whoever directed the metal men—was not an enemy. The robot had not actually attacked him—it had merely tried to subdue and capture. If he submitted peacefully...

But as the hurrying feet came closer a wave of cold horror chilled Mason, and on impulse he opened the nearest door and slipped through, closing the panel behind him. His eyes examined the room as he heard the robots race past. And, almost, Mason cried out in amazement, as, for the first time, he saw the woman who was called Nirvor—the Silver Priestess!

CHAPTER TWO
The Woman Out of Time

Mason stood on a low balcony, from which a sloping ramp led down to a broad, low-ceilinged room, lazy and perfumed with musky incense. Furs and rugs carpeted the floor. Below him, in the center of the chamber, was an altar, low and square, from which a flower of flame blossomed. Gleaming with cold silver radiance, it cast flickering gleams over the two huge beasts that stood beside the altar—two leopards, stretched in sinuous ease.

One leopard of polished ebony...

One white as the fabled gates of ivory through which, legends say, evil dreams pour from the Hell-city Dis to torment men's sleep...

Two leopards, brilliant green eyes intent on the woman who crouched before the flaming altar, a woman such as Mason had never seen before!

She was like a silver statue, exquisitely molded, her slender body half revealed by a lacy silken robe of black. Long unbound hair, moon-silver, drifted about her ivory shoulders. Her face Mason could not see; the woman knelt before the altar, and her voice, murmuring sorcerous music, whispered words in a tongue completely unfamiliar to the man.

And the pale fires seethed up coldly, whispering. The leopards watched unmoving. The woman's voice rose to a shrill, high keening.

"*Ohe, ohe!*" She spoke in the Semite tongue now, and Mason understood the words. "My city and my people and my kingdom! Ruined and fallen, and the beasts of the forest walk in the lonely streets of Corinoor...*ohe!*" The woman mourned, her hair falling loose about her face. With a sudden gesture she sprang erect, ripped her robe in tattered shreds from her body. For a moment her nude form was silhouetted against the milky fires, and Mason caught his breath at sight of the woman's undraped loveliness, the sleek perfection of limbs and torso, lithe as the forms of the watching leopards. Then the woman crouched down in utter self-abasement before the altar, her hands outstretched in appeal.

"Soon, let it be soon," her voice sobbed. "Let the Master succeed and bring power again to Corinoor…dead and lovely Corinoor. I, queen and priestess of Corinoor, ask this of you, like the meanest slave, naked and abased… Selene, mighty, Selene, turn your face again toward my people!"

Silence, and the soft whisper of the moon-fires. The leopards were statue-still. Their cold green eyes dwelt enigmatically on the woman.

Mason felt a queer chill touch him. Once more the eerie mystery of this haunted city shadowed him. He made a swift involuntary movement; one of the leopards coughed, sprang up on alert feet. The white leopard remained quiet, but the black one stalked forward, eyes intent on Mason. And there was something disturbingly strange about those eyes, the man realized—an intelligence that was more than a beast should possess.

The woman leaped up in one quick movement, stood staring, red lips parted. Mason felt his throat tighten at sight of her loveliness. Her eyes were deep pools of jet. And, perhaps, she read something of Mason's undisguised admiration, for the lips curved in a smile, and the low voice called a command.

"Bokya! To me!"

The black leopard halted, one paw lifted. Growling softly, it returned to the woman's side. She made a peremptory gesture.

Obeying, Mason walked forward down the ramp. His heart was thudding madly as he drew closer to the woman's pale beauty, and a pulse of passion was beating in his temples. She was Aphrodite, goddess of love and all delight…

Something he read in her eyes made Mason halt.

Beauty was there, yes. But there was something else, something coldly alien and dreadful, that seemed to lurk hidden in those cryptic depths, a quality of soul-lessness that sent a shock of repulsion tingling through Mason. But before he could speak a thudding of racing feet sounded near by.

In Mason's apprehensive glance at the door the woman read something of the truth. For a long moment she stood silent; then…

"In here," she whispered in Semite. "Make no sound!"

She bent, touched the altar. The pale fires died. The altar was a bare block of dark stone. At the woman's urging Mason mounted upon it hesitantly, stood rigid. Then, abruptly regretting his move, he made as though to leap down.

He was too late. The moon-flames sprang up, crackling softly. All around Mason now was a wall of silver fire, hiding the woman and all else from his eyes. Oddly there was no perceptible heat. Rather, a queer chill seemed to emanate from the weird flames. Slowly Mason relaxed, realizing that he was in no immediate danger. Yet why had the woman helped him?

Voices came from beyond the altar. Someone he could not see was speaking—questioning, demanding. The woman's voice answered. Then, for a time there was silence.

Again the moon-flame; died. The room was empty, save for the leopards and the woman. She had cast a robe of white fur about her shoulders. Laughing a little, she beckoned Mason.

"One of the Master's servants," she said. "He was searching for you. I sent him away. You're safe—for a while, at least." Mason got down from the altar, with a wary glance at the leopards. But, save for a growl or two, they paid him no heed. He came close to the woman and said in Semite:

"You have my thanks, O goddess who rules men's hearts." Her face clouded at the flowery phrase. "Do not speak of goddesses. I worship one goddess—and I have fear of her, but no love. Well—what is your name?"

"Mason."

"Mason—yes. And I am Nirvor. I do not think you have been in Al Bekr long, eh?"

"Half an hour at most. You're the first human being I've seen, except—" Some indefinable instinct of caution made Mason stop before he mentioned the Sumerian. Nirvor's jet eyes grew keen.

"Except—?"

"The robots."

The woman smiled slightly. "What year do you come from?"

Mason caught his breath. This confirmed his wild guesses. The power of the twin monoliths had flung him into time— as he had thought. Fighting back his questions, he said as calmly as he could, "1939." And added, as an afterthought, "A.D."

"Then—as you would reckon it—I come from 2150, long in your future. I was caught by the time trap, as you were, and drawn back to this dawn-era before Egypt or Rome ever sprang from the dust. And here, in long-forgotten Al Bekr, I found—the Master."

Nirvor watched, but Mason made no sign. She said, "You have not seen him yet?"

"No. Who is he?"

"He is from the future—my future as well as yours. Five thousand years later than your time-sector—nearly ten thousand years from now, in Earth's dusk. He built the time projector, and with its aid traveled back to this almost prehistoric city. The projector was wrecked, but the Master determined to rebuild it. He conquered Al Bekr, and with the robots he made, turned it into a city of science. Then he set to work to repair the projector."

"How did you get here?" Mason asked. "I don't see—"

"The twin monoliths have in them atomic power, and when this is released, the time-warp is set in operation. Any object within their field of force is hurled into time. This is true now, or a million years from now. Mason, the green time-towers that the Master builds now will stand in this valley when Al Bekr is a lifeless wilderness. They will stand in your day, and they will stand in mine, and through the ages, holding within them the power of time travel. Once in a thousand years, perhaps, a human being will be within range of the towers when the force is released, perhaps by lightning, as it was when I was captured. My caravan had camped beneath the palms of an oasis in the valley of Al Bekr, and I, wandering in the storm, sleepless, was between the green towers when lightning struck. I was drawn back through time to the period in which the projector first existed—now, when the Master rules Al Bekr."

Mason's mind was busy with this explanation. He said, "Are we the only ones who have been captured by the monoliths?"

"You and I, and the Master—and one other. He—" Nirvor hesitated. "We shall not speak of him." She sank down beside the altar, stretching like a cat. The leopards watched silently. Nirvor eyed Mason from half-lowered lids, pale ash-blonde lashes sweeping her cheeks.

"It has been lonely here," she said. "Sit down, Mason."

He obeyed. The woman went on.

"Long and long have I waited. The Master has promised to return me to my own time, to aid me in rebuilding my dead city, marble Corinoor. But in the meantime I wait among these barbarians—I wait, and I worship Selene, and my leopards guard me…they, too, were captured by the time-towers when I was." A slim hand caressed the furry jaw of the black beast. From half-closed eyes it peered at her, growling softly.

"They are wise, Mason—Bokya and Valesta. Long before Corinoor fell, our scientists had evolved certain creatures, and the sacred leopards were wisest of all. Remember, Mason—Bokya and Valesta are very wise…"

With a lithe movement Nirvor moved close to Mason. She whispered, "But I grow tired of wisdom. I am—woman.

Slim arms stole about Mason's neck. Nirvor's perfumed breath was warm in me man's nostrils, a perfumed madness that mounted headily to his brain. His throat was dry and clamped.

He bent his head, pressed his lips against Nirvor's scarlet ones. When he drew back he was trembling a little.

"Mason," the woman whispered. Her eyes met and locked with the man's. And, for the second time, Mason saw something alien in them.

A cold, cruel, distant something that made him draw back involuntarily, appalled by the subtle horror in Nirvor's eyes. Mason could not understand exactly what repulsed him; he was not to know this until much later. But he knew, with a dreadful certainty, that the woman was a Horror…

Her lips were suddenly twisted with menace. But she choked back a flood of words, stood up, and Mason stood up beside her. This time she did not let her gaze meet the man's. She lifted pale hands to her throat, unbuckled the clasp that held the robe. It slipped down rustling to her feet.

21

Mason tried to look away—and found he could not. Nirvor might be evil—but she was a goddess indeed, a marble Galatea sprung to life and instinct with passion. She stepped forward; her bare arms went about Mason's neck.

Setting his jaw, he tore them free, thrust the woman back. Remembrance of the inexplicable strangeness in Nirvor's eyes was too strong.

"You say you come from the future," Mason whispered, gripping the woman's wrists. "And just how do I know what—creatures—may exist then?"

She caught the implication. Fury blazed in the jet eyes. She tore free, sprang back, and shrilled an angry command.

"Slay him, Bokya—*slay!*

The black leopard sprang erect. It crouched, stalking slowly toward Mason.

A voice said sharply, "This man is the Master's, Nirvor. Slay him—and you die!"

CHAPTER THREE
Vengeance of the Master

Mason turned his head, saw Erech, the Sumerian, at the door.

The man came striding swiftly down the ramp, his cold eyes harsh.

"Hear me? Nirvor—"

The silver priestess hissed shrilly. The black leopard hesitated, slunk back to its place. Nirvor turned blazing eyes on the Sumerian.

"Since when have *you* commanded *me?*"

"I speak for the Master," Erech said smoothly, with an undertone of faint mockery. "And I do not think that even you care to defy him."

With an angry gesture Nirvor turned away, touched the altar. Again the pallid moon-fires sprang up. The Sumerian said, "I shall not speak of this episode to Greddar Klon. Nor would I advise you to do so."

The priestess made no reply, and Erech gripped Mason's arm, nodding toward the door. Silently Mason followed the other. Once they were in the corridor Erech blew out a long breath of relief.

"She's a demon, Ma-zhon—she and her familiars, those giant cats. Come along!" He pulled Mason with him till they reached the Sumerian's apartment. There, safely ensconced on furs, Erech grinned wryly.

"I thought the metal men had you. But you're not safe yet. Unless you want to take your chances with the Master—"

"Why should he harm me?" Mason asked, without much assurance.

"Well, there was another man who came as you did, out of nothing—a man named Murdach. He's in the vaults, chained and captive. I don't know why. True, Greddar Klon may not chain *you*—"

"I'd rather not make the experiment," Mason said. "But doesn't the Master know I'm here?"

"He isn't sure. Nirvor won't betray you, for that would mean betraying herself. I think you can hide in Al Bekr for a while, anyway. Its easy to find a white camel in a herd, but if it's dyed brown—" The Sumerian got up, found a length of cloth and a light cloak. "You'd best wear these."

Mason nodded. "When in Rome," he observed, but the other only stared. Then he remembered—Rome would not be born for thousands of years. Quickly Mason stripped, fashioned himself a loincloth, threw the cloak over his shoulders. Erech handed him a dagger. "I have no better weapon," he apologized. "My scimitar I need myself."

He led the way out into the passage, talking as he walked. "As for the Master, I don't know where he came from. Once Al Bekr was a paradise. Then Greddar Klon came, and with his magic enslaved us all. I was visiting Al Bekr when he arrived, having had occasion to flee Nippur." Diabolic mirth tinged his grim face for a moment.

"When my caravan got here. Alasa ruled. Then suddenly Greddar Klon came. I did not see that. Some say he sprang out of empty air, in broad daylight He made himself ruler, took Alasa as hostage, and keeps her imprisoned. He has made this into a city of fear. Look about you!" Erech flung out an arm at the green-lit corridor. "Al Bekr was not unduly beautiful before, but now it's like living underground with devils! Well, cities are no places for men anyway. If I—but none can escape. Some have tried, and died. Greddar Klon's slaves are everywhere."

The passage broadened. Behind them came quick footsteps. Mason felt the Sumerian nudge him. Racing past came a metal robot. If it saw them, it gave no heed. From the distance came the thudding tramp of many feet. The clanging note of a bell rang out.

Erech cursed. His eyes rolled, as though seeking a way of escape. More robots passed them. Mason gripped his dagger.

"No!" The Sumerian seized his wrist, pulled his hand from the weapon. His voice was low and urgent. "There's danger, but we may escape. Come!" He quickened his footsteps.

The metal men moved on, arm-tentacles swinging, bulging eyes astare. The clatter of their footsteps filled the passage. The bell clanged out again.

"It summons the city to the Council Room," Erech said. "All must be there. We've no chance to find a hiding place for you now. We must wait…"

Five minutes later they emerged into a great high-ceilinged room. It was vast, awe-inspiring in its bare hugeness. It was of white stone, windowless, lit with the inevitable green-glowing bars. Tunnel mouths ringed the walls. A multitude of men and women, a few children, were pouring from the passages.

Guided by Erech, Mason joined the rest. At one end of the great chamber was a raised dais, bare save for a silvery metal ovoid that hung in the air, apparently without support. It was perhaps seven feet long. Strangely it reminded Mason of a coffin. At sight of it he felt Erech grow tense beside him.

The room was filling with a surging multitude, brown-faced, furtive-eyed. They spoke in hushed tones among themselves, casting occasional quick glances toward the dais. To Mason it was strange indeed to hear the low mutterings of a language that no longer existed save among a few scholars—in his time, at least.

From the high ceiling a black disk dropped. Its descent was arrested, and it hung swaying above the crowd. The whisperings died into silence.

Two robots, side by side, emerged from a tunnel mouth beyond the dais. At their heels came rolling something like a great metal sphere, with the top sliced off—a huge hollow cup. Over its edge Mason saw a swollen, blue-veined baldhead, bulbous and hideous a monstrously bloated caricature of a human skull. Two sharp, beady eyes peered out intently from beneath that tremendous brain case.

Mason cast a sidelong glance at the Sumerian. Erech's eyes were cynical—yet they were troubled, too. Mason realized that the warrior's half-contempt for the Master had been not quite real—that it masked an uneasy, reluctant fear of Greddar Klon. To Erech, the Master must appear like some monstrous baroque, for he did not realize or understand, as did Mason, that with the passing of hundreds of thousands of years the human race would evolve into beings like the strange man on the dais.

Slowly the car rolled on behind the robots. A pale, slender hand, with elongated, tentacular fingers, writhed into view above the edge of the cup. The robots paused on the dais, and the car wheeled between them to lace the audience, among which, Mason saw, other robots stood like guards. A murmur went up from the throng.

"The Master!"

Mason lifted a quizzical eyebrow. He could understand now how Greddar Klon maintained his rule over the superstitious natives of Al Bekr, playing on their fear of the unknown. The entire auditorium, he saw suddenly, was like a huge theatre, cunningly arranged to impress the beholder with its mystery, its strangeness. Mason might find danger in the formidable science of Greddar Klon—but this mummery he could recognize and discount. Somehow he did not feel so utterly lost and helpless now.

The Master lifted a slender hand, and the throngs knelt.

Mason found a position behind a fat, shaven-headed man in a woolen cloak.

From the black disk dangling overhead came a flat, metallic voice. Mason glanced up slightly, cautiously. The apparatus—a radio amplifier, probably—must be strange indeed to Erech and the others.

"I have imprisoned Alasa, your queen," the voice said emotionlessly. "For a long time she has been my hostage, ever since I learned she was plotting to revolt against me. I have warned you, people of Al Bekr, that at the first sign of another revolt she would die. Well—there has been no such attempt. That I grant."

The Master's inscrutable eyes roved over the kneeling throng. Mason looked down quickly as the probing glance moved toward him. Again the toneless voice sounded.

"The prison of Alasa has been in plain view, as a warning. Yet it was forbidden to touch it. That command has not been obeyed."

Greddar Klon's head bent for a moment. A robot appeared in the tunnel mouth behind the dais, a tentacle-arm curled about the neck of a girl who walked beside it—a girl of perhaps twenty, her dark eyes distended, her hair matted with dried blood. She wore a plain white robe, torn and stained.

The metallic ovoid that hung above the dais dropped lower. The silvery sheen changed. Over its surface a shimmering play of color crawled. It became transparent as glass.

Within it was a girl.

Mason felt the Sumerian nudge him. "Alasa—our ruler," Erech whispered.

She lay within the transparent coffin, eyes closed, her dark hair falling in ringlets about an ivory, piquant face, and there was a strangely elfin beauty about her, enhanced by the close-fitting green garment she wore. Mason caught his breath, staring with his eyes. A scarcely noticeable movement went through the throng.

"It is death to touch Alasa's prison," the disk said coldly. "Let no one turn away his eyes."

Robots held the white-robed girl firmly. Others brought forward a curious appliance. Swiftly they ripped away the single garment, baring the captive's slim body in utter nudity. She cried out, fought vainly to escape.

But the robots were too strong. Dozens of circular disks, transparent as glass, were pressed against the girl's flesh, clinging apparently by suction. Flexible tubes led from them to a bulky machine on the dais.

A movement nearby drew Mason's attention. A man had risen to his feet, a brawny warrior with gray-streaked beard who was staring fascinated at the spectacle. Mason, following his gaze, felt cold horror touch him.

The girl on the dais was—changing! The skin beneath the innumerable glass cups grew red and inflamed. She screamed in agony, writhing against the metallic arms of the robots. Her naked body was no longer white—it was covered with dozens of crimson disks.

Mason understood. The air within the glass cups was being pumped out; powerful suction was wrenching at the girl's flesh.

There were little beads of perspiration on Erech's face. The Sumerian's jaw was grimly set, but he could not disguise the fear in his eyes. Under cover of the low murmur that filled the room Mason muttered, "It's trickery, Erech."

The Sumerian turned doubtful eyes upon him, glanced back swiftly to the dais. From the corner of his mouth he whispered, "You are wrong, Ma-zhon. This is not the first time it has happened. I—I do not like being afraid, Mazhon!"

The girl shrieked, her voice knife-edged with pain. The frightful suction tore at her flesh. Blood spurted into the glass cups. Nerves and veins and arteries were ripped into ghastly chaos. Her body became a shapeless mass of puffy, bleeding meat.

Someone shouted. Mason turned his head in time to see a spear flash through the air, hurled by the graybeard he had already noticed. Like a white flame the weapon flashed through the room, raced at the Master—and rebounded, fell clattering to the stones!

A beam of yellow light darted out from the dais. There was a shrill scream as the ray impinged on tender skin. It swung toward the graybeard. The man shouted, toppled back, his face a blackened cindery mass. "Beware!" the disk roared. "Beware the vengeance of the Master!"

"I knew him," the Sumerian muttered. "It was his daughter whom the Master slew just now—" He stopped as the murmuring of the throng suddenly died away.

In the stillness the voice of the black disk sounded unnaturally loud. "Let Nine-Seven-Four come forward," it said. Erech drew in his breath sharply.

Then, without a glance at Mason, the Sumerian rose and strode toward the dais. Just before he reached it he came to a stop, facing the Master.

"Where is the stranger who was in your quarters?" The voice came from Greddar Klon's thin lips, not from the amplifying disk overhead.

Erech said loudly. "I do not know. He escaped from my quarters." Mason knew the words were intended for his own ears.

So, apparently, did Greddar Klon. The Master's voice rang out again flatly.

"I speak to you, stranger. Come forward."

Mason did not move. A robot stepped forward. Its tentacle-arm coiled about Erech's neck. The Sumerian's hand leaped to the hilt of his scimitar, and then fell away. Amazingly the toneless voice spoke—in English, oddly accented but recognizable.

"I—mean you no—harm Come forward, if you—wish to return to your own—time-sector."

Startled, Mason involuntarily made a movement, hesitated, and then stood up quickly. After all, he had no choice. The tentacle about Erech's neck silently warned him of the torture that would be inflicted on the Sumerian if the Master were not obeyed.

Mason hurried forward, the target of furtive glances, passing Erech without a word. The swarthy warrior stared straight ahead, his face immobile. Greddar Klon nodded, and the robot uncoiled its tentacle from Erech's neck, twined it instead about Mason's upper arm. There was no menace in the gesture—rather, it seemed as though the creature had taken his arm to guide him. Mason felt a gentle tug, and the robot urged him toward the tunnel mouth behind the dais. The weird, spherical metal head, with its strange, faceted eye, stared down at him blankly.

With a glance at Erech, Mason followed the robot past the still form of Alasa, motionless within her floating transparent prison. Again the elfin beauty of her caught at Mason's throat. Then the green-lit depths of a passage swallowed him...

He was taken to the great room of the two monoliths. There he waited, still with the cold tentacle curled about his arm, till the sound of tramping footsteps came. Into the huge chamber came the two guardian robots; behind them

Greddar Klon in his metal car. The Master stopped the vehicle, swung open a door, laboriously climbed out to the floor.

Now Mason had an opportunity to study the strange man a bit more closely. He was short, his body dwarfed but thickset, and the arms were slender, boneless, terminating in elongated fingers. The bowed legs were quite thick and appeared very strong. They had to be, in order to support that tremendous brain case. A close-fitting nearly black garment covered the stocky body, the shoulders of which scarcely came to Mason's waist. The dwarf's head was papery-white, blue-veined. Almost Mason could imagine it pulsated with the throb of the living brain within. The bones of the skull must be very thin—the thought stirred something in his mind.

The tiny, pointed jaw moved, and a shrill voice spoke in syllables Mason did not understand.

Mason said, in English, "I am sorry but I do not speak your tongue."

The other replied haltingly in the same language, "I—I know yours. I have studied—records—" He lapsed into pure Semite, speaking more fluently. "Let us speak the root tongue. I have had reason to speak it much of late, though at first it gave me great difficulty. You...you are from the future. So am I—but a future far later than yours." He nodded. The tentacle slowly unwound from Mason's arm. The robot paced away, then returned with a heap of furs. Greddar Klon dropped upon them, and the robot brought more furs, threw them in a heap beside Mason. He, too, sank down.

"Let me explain. In my day I built a time machine, a projector, which hurled me far back into the past. There was an error in my calculations, though, almost fatal. I had intended to move only a few days into the future. But the time current was very swift… I emerged in this ancient city. And I had no way of returning. My time projector was not, of course, in existence. It would not exist till I built it, far if the future."

The cold eyes dwelt enigmatically on Mason. "I rebuilt my device. This time—somewhat differently. For I do not wish to err again—I do not care to go back to the Pliocene, or on to a dying, airless world. I have not yet finished my experiments. Do you know why I have told you this?"

Mason shook his head. Cameos of muscle ridged on his jaw.

"Not friendliness—no. I want your brain. Your intelligence. The robots will obey—but they are mindless. There are certain delicate operations and calculations…in my own time I had capable assistants, but I cannot use these barbarians, of course. You can help me. Your mind is undeveloped, but the rudiments of scientific knowledge are there, I wish your aid."

He watched Mason for a few moments and then went on, "It is the only way in which you can return to your own time. Do not let emotion sway you. These people here are nothing to me. Nor are you, save that I can use you. Help me—or die."

The archeologist hesitated. He did not doubt that refusal would mean death, or at least torture. He must play for time…until he understood more of this alien, enigmatic world.

"Very well. I'll help you," Mason spoke weariedly.

"Good." Greddar Klon peered closely at Mason. "You are tired. You must sleep now, and when you are refreshed we can begin."

A robot came forward. It took Mason's arm, urged him toward a passage.

The voice of the Master came, flat and ominous. "Remember—I do not trust you. But I think you understand that treachery will mean your death!"

CHAPTER FOUR
The Conspirators

For seven hours Mason slept dreamlessly, on a mound of furs in one of the bare apartments of Al Bekr. Once he roused at an unfamiliar sound to go to the door and open it. Outside the portal one of the metal robots stood motionless on guard. Smiling wryly, Mason returned to his couch and relaxed in sleep.

The next time he awoke it was to find a hard, callused palm clamped over his mouth. Startled, he fought desperately for a moment, and then paused as he heard the urgent whisper of Erech.

"Quiet, Ma-zhon! Be silent!"

The Sumerian's swarthy face was glistening with sweat. He took his hand from Mason's mouth, said, "We must be quick. There's a journey you must make before the Master sends for you."

"The robot—" Mason nodded toward the door. Erech's thin lips broadened in a grin.

"I've taken care of him. With this—see?" He brought out from the folds of his cloak a curious egg-shaped contrivance, milkily luminescent. "I got it from Murdach."

Murdach! Mason remembered—the man from the future whom Greddar Klon had imprisoned in the vaults of Al Bekr.

"How—"

"Murdach is wise—and powerful, though he's in chains. I visited him—after the Master had punished me for hiding you." The Sumerian rubbed his back gingerly, wincing. "I do not love the lash's kiss—no! Well, I told Murdach of you, and he has made a plan. He gave me this weapon against the metal men, and asked me to bring you to him. And Alasa, too—for the Master intends to slay her."

"What are we waiting for?" Mason asked. He sprang lightly to his feet, moved toward the door. His hand strayed toward the dagger at his belt, but Erech merely chuckled.

"No danger—so long as we move quietly, Murdach's weapon is powerful."

The Sumerian opened the door. The robot stood silent across the threshold, its faceted eye blank and dull. It made no move as the two men passed it. Erech said:

"It's under a spell."

Mason lifted quizzical eyebrows. True, to the superstitious Sumerian this must seem magic indeed, but the cause of the robot's paralysis could be guessed. The egg-like weapon of Murdach, perhaps, emitted a ray, which temporarily short-circuited the energy that activated the robot. How long, Mason wondered, would the metal man remain thus?

"Come on," Erech said, leading the way along the corridor. Silently the archeologist followed. Through green-lit, empty tunnels they went swiftly, and at last came out into the great room of the dais, where Greddar Klon had tortured and killed the Semite girl before the assembled multitudes of Al Bekr. The chamber was vacant now, save for the glass coffin that hung in empty air. Erech ran lightly toward it, Mason at his heels.

From a tunnel mouth a robot came striding. The Sumerian flung up his arm, the luminous, enigmatic weapon of Murdach's gripped in his thick fingers. From the shining object a pencil-thin beam of light sprang out.

It struck the robot's body. It spread, crawling over the metal surface like liquid. Suddenly the robot was a glowing figure of living light.

The monster stopped in mid-stride, tentacles rigidly out-stretched. It stood frozen.

The light-beam died. Erech hid the weapon in his garments.

"Now for Alasa," he growled. "Murdach told me how to free her. If I can remember—"

The Sumerian touched the opaque coffin, ran his hand lightly over its surface. He cursed softly—and then caught his breath. Beneath his fingers something clicked; there was a high-pitched, strange sound, as though a violin string had abruptly broken.

The coffin sank down, opening as it dropped. Within it lay Alasa—unmoving, asleep.

Mason leaned forward, his eyes intent on the girl. Alasa's beauty seemed scarcely earthly as she lay there, and for a moment Mason feared that she would not awaken.

Then the long, dark lashes lifted; warmly golden eyes looked into the man's. In that gaze a queer understanding came, and Alasa—smiled. No longer goddess—but human indeed!

Fear came into her face. She arose with a lithe motion, and looked around with the wariness of a hunted thing. In Semite Mason said:

"Do not be afraid. We come to free you—not to harm."

Alasa eyed him doubtfully. The Sumerian said:

"That is true. You know me, I think—and you know how I fought when the Master first came."

For the first time Alasa spoke, her voice low, a little husky, as though her vocal cords had not been used for long. "Yes, I know you, Erech. I trust you. But—tell me, how long have I been in this prison."

"Thrice four moons," Erech said. "But come; we'll talk as we go. There's no time to waste." He turned to the coffin, closed it, lifted it into the air, where it hung unsuspended. "The Master may not discover you're gone for a while, anyhow."

36

The Sumerian led the way. He seemed thoroughly familiar with the intricate maze of Al Bekr, though more than once Alasa's eyes widened in wonder at sight of her transformed city. Glancing aside at her, Mason felt his pulse leap at the girl's strangely elfin beauty. Once she looked at him with undisguised curiosity.

"You are from a distant land, I think," she observed. "Men of Al Bekr are either strong or handsome, but seldom both. You are not very handsome." She chuckled, golden eyes lighting with mirth. "Yet I like you!"

Before Mason could answer a shadow flitted past in the distance. It was the white leopard of Nirvor. It paused, eyeing the group inscrutably. Mason felt a shiver crawl down his spine. The creature was only a beast, of course—yet in its stare was a deadly malignancy and a queer spark of intelligence...

The leopard slipped away and was gone. Erech whispered, "It is a demon. Bokya, the black one, is a killer— but white Valesta is like Malik Taus, peacock-devil of the eastern tribes. Hurry!"

The way led downward now, along steeply sloping ramps, deserted, lit by the pale green radiance. Once they encountered a robot, but Erech's ray-weapon swiftly reduced it to immobility. Down they went, into the hidden depths beneath lost Al Bekr...

And fear crept at Mason's heels, stalking him. A dread he could not suppress had risen within him ever since the white leopard had appeared. An inexplicable certainty that danger was drawing closer...

Without warning disaster struck. From the gloom of a side passage a black bolt of lightning sprang—the black leopard! Right at Erech's head it leaped, and the Sumerian would have died then beneath grinding fang had not Mason, almost without thought, lunged forward into the man's back, hurtling him aside. A razor claw raked Mason's arm. He felt fur brush his cheek, so close did death pass. Then the leopard seemed to turn in midair, green eyes blazing.

But Erech had drawn his scimitar. With fury no less than the beast's he crouched, teeth bared in a savage grin.

"Back, Ma-zhon! Guard Alasa! Your dagger is shorter than my blade—let me deal with this hell-spawn."

Mason thrust the girl behind him. He drew his dagger. The leopard advanced on Erech, tail switching erratically. And—

Darkness fell.

The green-growing bars blinked out. Intense blackness shrouded the passage.

The nearness of doom sent inspiration lancing into Mason's mind. He cried, "The weapon, Erech! Murdach's weapon—" Whether the ray would paralyze the leopard Mason did not know. But at least, the glowing egg would provide light—light enough so that the leopard could not kill unseen in the blackness.

Whether Erech heard Mason did not know. The floor trembled beneath his feet. It shuddered and sank down as he fought for footing. He felt Alasa's soft body cannon into his, and then the two of them were plummeting down into the abyss.

They did not fall far, and a mound of furs saved them from injury. In the stygian gloom Mason heard the girl's unsteady breathing. He put out an exploring hand, touched the warm softness of an arm.

"Are you all right," Mason asked.

"I think so. But—Erech?"

Mason called the Sumerian's name. There was no response.

Light blazed into the room.

They were in a tiny cell, twelve feet square or less, walled and roofed with bare metal. Mason stood up, gripping his dagger.

A voice said mockingly, "Though Bokya fail—I do not. I am wiser than my leopard."

The voice of Nirvor! The Silver Priestess!

Mason looked around quickly. The unseen woman laughed softly.

"You cannot escape, either of you. You will die. Nor will the Master knew I slew you. For when the centaur feeds, he leaves not even bones."

Even at that moment Mason found time to wonder why Nivor bore him such hatred. Then he remembered his words and his shocked revulsion at the alien horror he had sensed in the eyes of the Silver Priestess. Nirvor remembered—and, to her, the offence was beyond forgiveness.

"I followed you," the cool voice went on, "till you reached the trap above the centaur's den. If the Master is too confident to guard himself against treachery, I shall guard him. For Greddar Klon has promised to bring back the glories of Corinoor under Selene, and you, who are his enemies, shall die—now!"

The floor tilted sharply. Once more Mason and Alasa dropped through space, alighting sprawled on a carpet of crackling straw. They were in a dim-lit chamber, high-roofed and huge. It seemed empty, though a black huddle loomed in a far corner.

Nirvor's voice came again. "Soon the centaur will waken. When you see him, pay homage to the Master's skill. For the centaur was once a man of Al Bekr, a fool and a murderer, who was bestialized in body and brain by Greddar Klon's science. He is not fed often. Nor are maidens often thrown into his den. And he is still partly human…" Ironic laughter died away into silence. Mason glanced at Alasa's white face.

"Buck up," he said, lapsing into English, and then in Semite, "Have courage. We're not dead yet."

The girl's lips were pale. "Yet I fear—this is magic!"

"I'm quite a sorcerer myself," Mason jested with an assurance he did not feel. He had noticed that the dark bulk in the corner was stirring. It arose. Slowly it came forward into the light...

Icy horror chilled the man A centaur—living, breathing, alive—stood before him, a monster out of mythology sprung to sudden life. The Master's surgery had created it, Mason told himself, yet he could not force down his repulsion. The creature was monstrous!

It had the body of a beast, a dun horse, all caked and smeared with filth. From the shoulders grew the torso and arms of a man, hairy and knotted with great muscles. The head was human, and yet, in some indefinable manner—bestialized. There was no intelligence in the shallow eyes, but a pale shining of dull hatred and menace.

The eyes flickered over him, swung to the girl. Light flared within them. The monster's loose, slobbering mouth twitched. It mouthed unintelligible sounds. The thick arms swung up. It pranced forward.

"Stay behind me," Mason said curtly. The dagger's hilt was cold in his hand. He lifted the weapon.

The centaur hesitated, looking down on the man. It seemed to sink down, crouching. And then it leaped.

It bounded forward, front hoofs flying, bellowing rage. As that gigantic mountain of flesh crashed down Mason thrust up desperately with the dagger. Whether his blow found a mark he did not know; a hoof smashed against his head, a glancing blow that sent him hurtling back, stunned. He fell in a limp heap on the straw.

Blackness surged up. Frantically he fought it back. His head was a blinding, throbbing ache of red agony, and when he forced open his eyes, he could not focus them properly.

Alasa's scream brought Mason back to full consciousness.

Unable to move, his muscles water-weak, he lay staring at the horror before him. The man-beast had gripped the girl in its hairy arms. The shallow eyes glared at her. One taloned hand swept out, snatched Alasa's garment, and ripped it brutally away.

Frantically Mason battled his overpowering weakness, the sickening dizziness that nauseated him. The centaur bellowed mad laughter.

And again the scream of Alasa came—terrified, hopeless!

CHAPTER FIVE
Madness of the Centaur

The centaur's monstrous head bent; watery orbs avidly dwelt on the girl's nudity. She struck out vainly, her nails ripping at the creature's face. Though blood came, the centaur paid no attention to its wounds.

Mason managed to crawl dizzily to his feet. The dagger lay glinting in the straw near him. He bent, picked it up. He turned toward the man-beast.

Alasa lay pale and motionless in the centaur's arms. The monster had no other thought than the girl. Its eyes were glaring and bloodshot. Spittle drooled from the sagging mouth. It did not see Mason as he crept forward.

The man had but one chance, and he knew it. Silently he stole up behind the beast. At the last moment the centaur sensed danger, started to whirl, roaring menace.

Mason's arm slashed down. The dagger ripped into the centaur's throat, slicing through skin and flesh and cartilage. A great gout of blood burst out, spattering the nude girl with scarlet.

With a deafening scream of agony the centaur dropped Alasa. Its hands clawed up to the ruined throat. It plunged at Mason.

He managed to dodge, though flying hoofs grazed his side. As the creature lunged past Mason put all his strength into a desperate leap. He felt iron-hard flesh under him, came down on the centaur's back, his arms locked about the monster's throat. The dagger was still in his hand.

The beast-man went berserk. Screaming, it flung back its hands, seeking its prey.

The taloned fingers sought Mason's eyes.

The man ripped out blindly with the dagger. He felt himself flung through the air, fell heavily on his side, rolling over and over. Clashing hoofs thundered past. Swaying, Mason sprang up—and halted, staring.

The centaur was blind. The dagger's chance stroke had ripped across its eyeballs, slashing them open. The beast-face was veiled with blood. And if the monster had been enraged before—now it was a demon incarnate!

Blind and dying, it shrieked mad rage and murder-lust. Hoofs grinding down viciously on the straw, great arms swinging, the centaur drove around the den, hunting the man who had slain it. Mason saw Alasa lying near by. He dashed toward her, lifted her nude body in his arms. He staggered into a corner, and the centaur flashed past him like a Juggernaut.

It was a mad, fantastic game they played there, with the dying monster blindly seeking prey, and with Mason, carrying the girl, dodging and waiting alternately, his breath a raw, singeing flame in his throat. All at once the centaur grew still, its bloody arms hanging laxly, blind head lifted questingly as it listened.

The creature stiffened as the girl in Mason's arms moaned and stirred. Guided by the sound, it sprang forward...

And dropped—dead! It rolled in a gory, shapeless huddle over and over on the straw, the great wound in the throat ceasing to bleed as the mighty beast-heart slowed and stopped. It lay quiescent, its dreadful life ended forever.

Reaction shook Mason. Dizzily he lowered the girl to the ground, relaxed beside her, weak and sick. But after a moment he rallied his strength and turned to Alasa. She was still and white as a marble statue, her pale body splotched with the centaur's blood. Mason's throat was suddenly dry. Was she even alive?

Swiftly he chafed her arms, striving to bring her back to consciousness. And at last the girl's lashes lifted; golden eyes looked into Mason's, wide and fearful. With a shuddering little cry Alasa clung to the man, no longer the queen of a mighty city, but a girl, frightened and thoroughly human. Involuntarily Mason bent his head, kissed the soft hollow of her throat, her rounded shoulders.

A flush turned Alasa's face rosy. She drew away, freed herself.

"There ought to be a way out of here," Mason said abruptly, unsteadily. "The Master depended on the centaur's killing his victims. There'd be no need to make this place a real prison. I—I'll look around."

In a corner Mason found a tiny stream that emerged from a hole in the wall and ran along a channel to disappear into a drain. Where the stream emerged there was a tube that slanted up into the darkness. It did not look inviting, but after a careful search of the den Mason realized that it was the only means of egress.

"Want to try it, Alasa?" he asked. The girl had been watching him, and now she nodded and came to his side. "I'll go first," Mason offered. "If I can get through you'll be able to."

He fell on hand and knees, crept into the hole. The water was not deep. It flowed beneath him, icy-cold and murmuring softly.

Mason was in a tunnel, a tube barely wider than the width of his shoulders, so smooth that at times he almost lost his footing. If the slope grew much steeper, he knew, it would be impossible to mount it. Behind him he heard the girl, her breathing soft and uneven.

The faint light that filtered from behind them grew dim and died away entirely. They clambered through utter darkness.

Interminable journey through the hidden heart of Al Bekr! More than once Mason felt chill despair touch him, but he knew that to retrace his steps would be useless, probably fatal. In the den of the centaur they would be at the mercy of Nirvor and the Master, but here they had at least a chance, though a slim one.

The tube grew level again. Fumbling in the dark, Mason felt emptiness beside him. The sound of falling water came. He realized that the tunnel branched here, forking into two tubes up one of which they had climbed. He called, "Not too fast, Alasa! Take hold of my foot—"

Slowly they edged past the unseen abyss. Then forward again, on hands and knees that were raw and bleeding—on and on interminably. Until, at last, a faint greenish glow heartened Mason. He increased his pace.

A mesh grating was set in the tube above him. He fumbled with it vainly. It was fast. With a word to the girl, Mason braced himself, thrusting his back against the barrier. Veins bulged in his forehead as he strained to lift it.

There was a faint creaking, but the grating did not give. Mason rested, and then tried again. This time he managed to burst open the grated metal.

Warily he lifted his head through the gap, peering around. They were in a room, green-lit and vacant, filled with water tubes, pumps, unfamiliar machinery. Mason wriggled out through the gap he had made, helped Alasa climb free. Both of them were drenched and shuddering with cold.

"So far, so good," Mason said grimly. "Do you know where we are?"

The girl shook her head. Dark hair clung damply to her bare shoulders. "This city is strange to me also. I don't know how we can escape—or where we can hide."

"Well, we can't stay here," Mason grunted. "Come along." He led the way to a tunnel-mouth in the wall. Warily they hurried along it. Al Bekr was still sleeping—but it would awaken soon, Mason thought. Moreover, if they encountered one of the robot guards, they no longer had Murdach's paralysis-weapon.

Twice they saw robots in the distance, but managed to evade them. It seemed hours later when, hurrying along a green-lit corridor, Mason heard footsteps approaching. He stopped short.

Alasa's face was white. She whispered, "What—"

"We passed a door a minute ago," Mason said softly. "Come on!"

They ran back swiftly. The door was unlocked; Mason swung it open, revealing a tiny closet bristling with switches and apparatus. "In we go," he commanded. "Hope we don't electrocute ourselves."

The footsteps were louder. The two tumbled into the closet, and Mason drew the door shut. He had intended to leave a tiny crack for vision, but the panel swung closed with a click. In the darkness Mason fumbled for a latch. There was none.

The steps grew louder, hesitated, and faded in the distance. Mason could feel Alasa's warm breath on his cheek. He said quietly, "We can't get out. We're locked in."

The girl said nothing for a moment, and them came into his arms, shuddering with cold and fear, clinging to him. The touch of her cool flesh dried Mason's throat. He resisted for briefly—and then a flame of passion swept away his caution. His hands touched silken curves; he felt Alasa's soft lips. Their touch was like fire.

He drew the girl close. With a little sob she put slim arms about Mason's neck. Their lips merged, and a trembling shudder shook Alasa's body as she strained toward him.

The footsteps came again—and another sound that electrified Mason. Soft, furious oaths—in a voice he knew.

The voice of Erech!

The girl had heard it too. She drew away, unseen in the darkness. Mason called with quiet urgency:

"Erech! *Erech!*"

Silence. Then the Sumerian's low tones.

"Eh? Who's that?"

"Mason. And Alasa. In here—"

The door swung open. Erech stood wide-eyed, his mouth open. His cloak was ribboned, his swarthy chest bleeding in a dozen places.

"I've found you—El-lil be praised! I've been searching all Al Bekr—"

He whipped off his cloak, gave it to the girl. She nodded gratefully, wrapping it around her nude form.

"I've no cloak for you, Ma-zhon—but you'll be back in your apartment in a moment. What happened to you?"

Mason told him. The Sumerian whispered an oath. "That she-devil—Nirvor! You saved my life, Ma-zhon, when you cried out for me to use Murdach's weapon. It gave me enough light to beat off the leopard. I didn't kill it—but I gave the beast some wounds to lick." He grinned unpleasantly.

"Now listen, Ma-zhon—and you, Alasa. I went to Murdach. I told him what had happened. He said there would be no time for him to talk to you now. Al Bekr will awaken soon. If you lived—he said—give you this message. Alasa I will hide safely. You, Ma-zhon, must pretend to obey the Master. Work with him as he wishes. Try to learn his secrets. Murdach knows something of them, but not enough. Later Murdach will join his knowledge to yours, and the two of you—with my aid—may defeat Greddar Klon."

Mason nodded. "Okay. I mean—it is well, Erech. You say Alasa will be safe?"

"For a time. I know the hidden places of Al Bekr. We must hurry, Ma-zhon—" The Sumerian gave Mason explicit directions for returning to his apartment. "Go now. Swiftly. Obey the Master till you hear from me."

Alasa ran to the archeologist, her golden eyes anxious. "And you will guard yourself—for my sake?" She lifted her pale face, and...

Mason kissed her again. He heard the Sumerian whistle, shrill with astonishment. The girl turned to Erech, said imperiously, "Let us go. *Now!*"

Shrugging, Erech led Alasa along the corridor. His lips still fragrant with the honey-musk of the girl's kiss, Mason went in the opposite direction, smiling a little.

And soon he found his apartment. The robot guard still stood before the door, unmoving as Mason slipped within. He cleansed and bathed his wounds as well as he could, donned a cloak that would hide them from the Master's suspicious eyes. Then he relaxed on the mound of furs.

He slept, but not for long. The robot was beside him, gently gripping his arm, urging him to his feet. A little thrill of fear shook Mason. Had the Master discovered what had happened? Had Nirvor spoken?

No—the Silver Priestess would be silent, for her own sake. Reason told Mason that the Master would be merciless if he knew Nirvor had tried to kill the man Greddar Klon needed to aid him. With an assumption of nonchalance the archeologist accompanied the robot to the room of the green monoliths.

The Master was reclining on furs. He thrust a flask at Mason. "Drink," the shrill voice piped. "It is not a drug. Rather a food, neutralizing the toxins of weariness."

Mason drank. His fatigue dropped from him.

The Master made no reference to Alasa's escape, if he knew of it, which Mason did not think likely. He arose on his bowed legs.

"Now we shall begin!"

The ordeal started. And it was a racking and cruel one; Mason's brain had never worked so fast, and, despite the energizing effect of the liquid, a dull headache began to oppress him. He could only guess at much of the nature of the work he did. Remembering Erech's command, he tried to memorize his activities and those of Greddar Klon.

Under the Master's direction he moved levers, spun wheels, and sent light-rays impinging on huge machines. From time to time, at the dwarf's dictation, he made cryptic notations with a stylus upon a camera-shaped device on which a scroll was wound—a variation on a notebook. And, as Mason worked, a trickle of knowledge crept into his brain. He began to understand some of the machines and powers of the Master of Al Bekr.

Several times he had attempted to hand objects to the dwarf, and had felt an invisible solid repel his hands—a shell of energy, Greddar Klon explained, which protected him from danger. "An atomic mesh guarding my body, through the interstices of which I can breathe, but which cannot be penetrated otherwise—by weapons or rays." The cold eyes examined Mason impassively.

Remembering the spear that had rebounded from this invisible armor, the archeologist realized its necessity. And, as they worked, Mason noticed several of the transparent ovoids about, similar to the one that had imprisoned Alasa. Several were large, fully twenty feet long. "I use them for aerial travel when I have need to leave Al Bekr," the dwarf said.

One thing Mason learned was that the air pressure within these ovoids could be controlled—increased or decreased.

This he remembered, though at the time he did not realize the importance of the device.

"I have given the barbarians of Al Bekr comforts they never knew before," Greddar Klon said. "Of course, I built the city for my own comfort primarily, while I was working on my projector. But they will still have it when I'm gone, though they'll be unable to actuate the machines. Come."

He led the way to one of the ovoids—twenty feet long, of opaque silvery metal. Greddar Klon touched a stud, and a disk-shaped door swung open. He motioned Mason within, followed him. As he turned to the instrument panel Mason watched his movements closely. The walls of the ship shimmered, faded—became shadowy, transparent. The ovoid lifted, drove up.

They raced up swiftly beside the giant pillars. At their summit, between them, a platform had been constructed, and on this the ship alighted. At a dizzy height above the floor the work continued, amazingly intricate adjustments and calculations, which Mason did his best to understand. And presently the dwarf, his voice emotionless as ever, announced, "It is finished. There remains only one thing."

The two were within the ship, but now Greddar Klon opened the port. He pointed to a lever on the platform a dozen feet away. "Pull that over. Then return—swiftly!"

Mason obeyed. As he returned to the ship he caught a fleeting glance from the Master, curiously veiled, and wondered. The dwarf said, "I have improved my original projector. Watch."

Silently a pale shimmer of white flame began to spread in empty air between the summits of the green towers. Glowing filaments and tentacles, like tatters of some huge curtain, danced and fluttered, spreading, even closing the gap between the monoliths. The green light faded, fled back. In the white glare distorted shadows marched grotesquely on the distant walls.

"Before—I guessed at my destination in time. Now I can control it. The energy of the projector is being transmitted to this ship, giving it the power to move in time."

Now the white curtain was unbroken, flaming all around the ovoid's transparent walls. Mason's eyes ahead as he watched it.

Then it snapped out and vanished. It was gone.

Coldly Greddar Klon said, "It is ended. My experiment is finished—and successful."

He touched the control board. "One test, though. We'll move back in time—for one orbit of the Earth."

The ship trembled, swayed. And suddenly utter, stygian blackness fell, through which screamed the vibration of energy inconceivable!

CHAPTER SIX
Terror in Al Bekr

Before Mason could do more than catch his breath light came again. The ship had apparently not moved—yet the scene visible through the transparent walls was entirely different.

No longer were they in the room of the twin monoliths. The ship hung in empty air twenty feet above the roofs of a strange, archaic city. It was Al Bekr, Mason knew—but Al Bekr as it had been before the Master's arrival.

A city of roughly cut stone and mud-daubed huts, such a city as Babylon might have been before the days of its splendor—like Chaldean Ur before its ruin. Men and women moved quietly about the streets. They had not as yet glimpsed the ship hovering above.

"I am satisfied," the Master said. "I can control the time-change accurately. Now we return."

Again darkness. And again it lifted, to show the room of the green towers. Greddar Klon sent the ship drifting down to the distant floor.

"When are you going to start?" Mason asked. The cold eyes probed him.

"Tomorrow. You had best return to your apartment and rest. I will need your aid soon."

Mason turned to the opening port. He vaulted lightly down and went to a tunnel-mouth. But something he had read in the Master's glance made him wary. He lurked in the passage out of sight, waiting.

Nor had he long to wait. Presently a low, distant voice sounded.

"You sent for me, Greddar Klon."

The voice of Nirvor, the Silver Priestess.

And the Master's reply:

"All is ready. We can start now."

A pause. Then Nirvor said, "My leopards. I must get them."

Mason wiped his forehead. So Greddar Klon intended betrayal. He planned to return to the future with Nirvor, leaving Mason behind. Well—Mason would not have gone without Alasa; but the thought came to him: would it not be best thus? With Nirvor and Greddar Klon gone, Alasa could rule Al Bekr as before.

And then—what? Mason himself would be marooned in a long-forgotten time sector, together with Murdach, the man from the future. Perhaps Murdach could help. True, Mason had been ordered to obey the Master till he received word from the Sumerian, but this was an emergency.

If only he could find Erech! But he did not know where to look. Mason, about to turn away, was halted by Nirvor's return. He edged forward cautiously, listening to the priestess' soft laughter, and caught sight of the woman. She was moving toward the time-ship, the two leopards beside her. She entered it. The leopards sprang lithely through the portal. Greddar Klon followed.

What now? Indecision held Mason motionless. His impulse was to halt the Master, kill him if possible. But how? The atomic shield could not be penetrated by any weapon made by man. And there were the leopards...

The problem was solved for him. The ship suddenly grew hazy, a shimmering oval shadow. It faded and was gone.

Where the time-ship had been was nothing. It had been launched on its incredible journey into the future.

A hand gripped Mason's shoulder. He whirled to face Erech.

"Murdach sent me," the Sumerian said. "The Master's gone, eh?"

Mason nodded wordlessly. Suddenly Erech grinned.

"Good! That's what Murdach wanted. He sent me to watch you, to stop you from doing anything rash. There was no time before to warn you. Come along now. I've freed Murdach, with the aid of his magic weapon. He's with Alasa."

Mason was conscious of a heightening of his pulses as he followed the Sumerian along the corridor. The robots were not visible; Mason wondered what they would do without the Master's will to direct them.

Soon he was to find out, in a manner that would not be pleasant. No premonition of this came to him now as he paused with Erech before a metal door, followed the other over the threshold. In the bare room two people were standing, Alasa, and a slim, hawk-faced patrician figure who was, Mason knew, Murdach. The man from the future wore the remnants of a tattered leather uniform. His forehead, while high and broad, did not have the bulging malformation of Greddar Klon's. Red hair stood up stiffly, but of eyebrows and lashes he had no trace.

Murdach said, his voice smooth and velvety, "You've brought him. Good." Enigmatic black eyes regarded Mason intently.

"Greddar Klon's gone," the archeologist said, frowning. "You know that?"

"Yes. And that is well. He is out of the way, while we make our plans to follow him."

At the audacity of the scheme Mason's eyes widened. Murdach went on:

"You do not know Greddar Klon's plan. He intends to become the ruler of the greatest civilization ever erected. A cosmic pirate, traveling through all ages, picking the best brains and the mightiest scientific powers from ancient times to the furthermost future. He told me of this, and asked my aid. Mason—that is your name, eh? He plans to build his civilization in a time-sector that can offer little resistance. He has chosen your decade."

Mason caught his breath. "He can't—"

"He has the power, with the time-ship to aid him. When he has looted time, he'll halt in 1929, wipe out mankind, subjugating a few races into slavery, and rear his civilization there. My plan is to follow him, building another time-ship—and kill him if I can. Will you aid me?"

Mason nodded. "That goes without saying!" A nightmare vision rose up in the archeologist's mind; a vision of a world in which time had lost its meaning, a world cowering beneath the tremendous powers of Greddar Klon. He drew a deep breath. "Can you build the ship?"

"With your aid. That was why I told you to watch the Master as you helped him. In collaboration we can fit together the pieces of the puzzle."

Alasa put a slim hand on Mason's arm. "I'm going with you, of course."

"You can't," Mason told her. "There'll be danger, and lots of it."

She lifted an imperious head. "What of that? Greddar Klon put me to shame—enslaved me and slew my subjects. Also, you have saved me, and I pay my debts. I go with you!"

"And I, too," the Sumerian broke in. "I've a wish to try my scimitar on the Master's neck, when his magic isn't guarding him."

"No more argument," Murdach said. "They will accompany us, if they wish. They hate Greddar Klon—and hatred is sometimes a powerful weapon." He turned to the door, and the others followed. Mason slipped the girl's arm within his own, squeezing it reassuringly. Her golden eyes laughed up at him gaily. They might be going into deadly peril—but Alasa was not lacking in courage.

In the room of the green monoliths all was still. Quickly Murdach moved about, his keen black eyes taking in all that was to be seen. He indicated a twenty-foot ovoid nearby.

"We can use that for our time-ship," he said. "But it's necessary first to build up the atomic force Greddar Klon used. Do you remember how he used this ray-device?"

Mason explained as well as he was able. Murdach nodded with satisfaction and made hasty adjustments. Slowly, gradually, the brain of the man from the future duplicated the Master's experiments. Mason began to feel hope mounting within him.

He was beneath one of the monoliths, explaining a control board to Murdach, when the girl cried warning. Mason swung about. From a tunnel-mouth raced two robots, faceted eyes alight, arm-tentacles swinging. They made for the group under the time towers.

Swiftly Murdach brought up his egg-shaped weapon. From it the ray sprang out, stilling the robots with fantastic swiftness. They stood silent, unmoving. But from the passage came the thunder of racing feet.

Murdach bit his lips. "I was afraid of this," he whispered. "Greddar Klon foresaw that we might follow him. Before he left, he ordered his robots to kill us. I doubt if we'll have time now."

"Time?" It was the Sumerian, battle-lust in his eyes. He stooped, snatched up a huge sledgehammer. "Give Alasa your weapon, Murdach. You and Ma-zhon finish your task. We'll hold off those demons!"

Alasa snatched the ray-projector, raced toward the tunnel mouth, Erech at her heels. Murdach smiled grimly.

"Let us hurry. We may have a chance, after all."

Mason was frowning, looking around for a weapon. The other gripped his arm.

"You can best help by aiding me. We can't battle all the robots. Only if we get the time-ship completed can we escape."

A metal man lunged into view, silent and menacing. The ray-projector in Alasa's hand stilled him. But there were others—hundreds of them, pressing eagerly forward. Some the girl halted. Others fell victim to Erech.

The Sumerian roared red battle curses. The sledge rose and fell in sweeping, crashing blows, grinding the metal heads of the robots beneath its drive. But slowly the two were pressed back—slowly, inexorably.

Murdach's fingers flew, adjusting, testing. Mason stole a glance at the battling pair, and straightened, his breath hissing between his teeth as he saw Erech go down beneath a flailing tentacle. The archeologist leaped forward. The girl might hold back the robots for a moment—no longer.

Leaping over the Sumerian's body, Mason snatched up the sledge. He saw the featureless blank head of a robot looming before him. A tentacle slashed down, vicious and deadly. Mason swung the hammer in a great arc.

Metal sang under the blow. The robot fell away and was gone. But behind him came others. Erech sprang up, spitting blood.

"The hammer, Ma-zhon! Let me—"

Behind them came Murdach's urgent cry. "Come! It's finished!"

Mason gripped Alasa's hand, ran toward Murdach, half dragging the girl. Behind him Erech shouted triumphantly, and then followed. The robots came in pursuit with a dull thudding of swift feet.

Murdach was waiting at the port of the ship. He sprang back into the interior as Mason thrust the girl aboard, tumbling in after her, Erech behind him. The door clanged shut just as the robots reached the ovoid. With insensate, brainless fury they attacked the metallic walls.

White-faced, Murdach turned to the control board, sent the ship driving up. He lowered it gently on the platform at the summit of the twin monoliths.

"That lever," he said, pointing. "You moved that one?"

Mason nodded. "Shall I—"

"Yes."

The archeologist opened the port and slipped out. He glanced over the platform's edge to see the robots milling about aimlessly beneath. Then he moved the lever and raced back to the ship.

Breathlessly the four waited. Presently white flame fingered out from the monoliths. Silently it spread, lacing and interweaving, till the walls were a sea of pale flame.

And it died.

For a moment no one spoke.

"Think it'll work?" Mason asked shakily.

"It must!" But Murdach's voice was none too steady. Nevertheless he turned to the controls, fingering them tentatively. Though Mason had expected it, nevertheless he felt a shock when darkness blanketed them.

It lifted. The ship hung above a green oasis, with high palms growing about a pool. In the cloudless blue sky the sun blazed brilliantly. For miles around the oasis was a desolate wilderness of sand and rock.

Alasa whispered, "Our legends say Al Bekr was like this once, long and long ago."

"There was no oasis in my day," Mason said. "We've gone back into the past."

"Then we'll go forward again," Murdach smiled, his eyes no longer grim and cold. "All time lies before us."

"Gods!" said Erech hoarsely. "This is magic indeed!"

The girl touched Murdach's arm. "What of my people? The robots may slay them."

"No. Their energy must be renewed periodically, or they're lifeless and inanimate. Without Greddar Klon to do that, they'll run down—lose their life force. Your people are safe enough, Alasa."

"But my epoch isn't," Mason grunted. He was beginning to understand something of the incredible task before them. How could they find Greddar Klon in the vast immensity of time—and, if they succeeded in finding him, how could they defeat the super-science of the Master, augmented, perhaps, by the powers of a dozen future civilizations?

As though guessing his thought, Murdach said, "I can locate Greddar Klon easily enough. His ship causes a warp in the space-time continuum that instruments can detect. But as for fighting him—I would like to get aid first. We can best do that far in the future. Surely there must exist some weapon there that will destroy the Master…"

He touched the instrument board. Once more darkness blanketed them. Mason felt the girl's soft body huddle against him, and he put a protective arm about her. The Sumerian was cursing softly and fluently.

And the ship raced into time, into the cryptic twilight of Earth, driving blindly toward mystery and toward horror inconceivable!

CHAPTER SEVEN
In Time's Abyss

Light came. They hung a thousand feet above the black, sullen waters of a sea that stretched to the horizon. There was no sign of land. In a black, star-studded sky loomed a globe of dull silver, incredibly vast. Its diameter covered fully a third of the heavens.

Mason said uncomprehendingly, "The Moon—but it's close, Murdach—very close! How far in the future have we gone?"

Murdach's face was white. He eyed the instruments, reached out a tentative hand, withdrew it. Hesitating, he said, "Something is wrong. I did not know—"

"Wrong?" The Sumerian growled an oath. "You said you'd mastered this hell-chariot!"

"I—I thought I had. But it is abstruse—Greddar Klon came from a more advanced world than mine."

"We're not—" Mason felt oddly cold as he asked the question. "We're not marooned here, are we?"

Murdach's lips tightened. He gripped a lever, swung it over. His slim fingers danced over the control panel. Nothing happened.

"For a while, at least," he said at last. "I cannot send the machine into time. But soon I can discover what's wrong—at least I think so."

Alasa smiled, though her eyes were frightened golden pools. "Then do your best Murdach. The sooner you succeed, the sooner we'll find the Master."

"No, no," Murdach told her impatiently. "We'll find Greddar Klon in a certain time-sector. Whether we start now or in an hour or in fifty years will make no difference."

"Fifty years!" Erech's vulturine face was worried. "And in the meantime—what will we live on? What will we eat?"

Ten hours later the question reoccurred. Both Murdach and Mason were haggard and red-eyed from their calculations and their study of the time-ship's principles. The former said at last, "How long this will take I don't know. We'd better find food. Too bad we took none with us."

"Where?" the Sumerian asked. He glanced around expressively at the bleak, lonely expanse of sea and Moon-filled sky. "I think Ran, the goddess of the Northmen, has claimed the world for her own. The ocean-goddess..."

"There'll be land," Mason said rather hopelessly as Murdach sent the ship lancing through the air. "If we go far enough."

But it was no long distance to the shore—a flat, barren plain of grayish sandy soil, eroded to a horizontal monotony by the unceasing action of wind and wave. No mountains were visible. Only the depressingly drab land, stretching away to a dark horizon. And there was no life. No animals, no vegetation; a chill emptiness that seemed to have no end. The dreadful loneliness of it made Mason shudder a little.

"Is this the end?" he wondered softly, aloud. "The end of all Earth?"

Sensing his mood, through not comprehending the reason for it, Alasa came close, gripped his arm with slim fingers. "We'll find food," she said. "Somewhere."

"We don't need to worry about water, anyway," he grunted.

"It's easy to distill that. And there's—"

"*Hai!*" Erech shouted, pointing, his pale eyes ablaze. "Men—see? There—"

Below them, a little to the left of the drifting ship, a great, jagged crack loomed in the plain. There was movement around it, life—vague figures that were busy in the unchanging silvery twilight of a dying Earth.

"Men?" Murdach whispered. "No…"

Nor were they men. As the ship slanted down Mason was able to make out the forms of the strange creatures. Vaguely anthropoid in outline, there was something curiously alien about these people of a dying world.

"Shall we land?" Murdach asked.

Mason nodded. "Might as well. If they show signs of fight, we can get away in a hurry."

The craft grounded with scarcely a jar near the great crack in the ground. Confusion was evident among the creatures. They retreated, in hurried confusion, and then a group of four advanced slowly. Through the transparent walls Mason scrutinized them with interest.

They were perhaps eight feet tall, with a tangle of tentacles that propelled them swiftly forward. Other tentacles swung from the thick, bulging trunk. The head was small, round, and without features—a smooth knob, covered with glistening scales. The bodies were covered with pale, pinkish skin that did not resemble human flesh.

Murdach said, "They are—plants!"

Plant-men! Amazing people of this lost time-sector! Yet evolution seeks to perfect all forms of life, to adapt it perfectly to its environment. In earlier days trees had no need to move from their places, Mason knew, for their food was constantly supplied from the ground itself. With the passing of slow eons perhaps that food had been depleted; limbs and branches had stretched out slowly gropingly, hungrily. Painfully a tree had uprooted itself. The mutant had given life to others. And now, free of age-old shackles, Mason saw the plant-men, and fought down his unreasoning horror at the sight.

Murdach said, "Listen! I think they're speaking to us—"

"Speaking?"

"With their minds. They've developed telepathy. Don't you feel some sort of message?"

"I do," Alasa broke in. "They're curious. They want to know who we are."

Mason nodded. "I don't think they're dangerous." He opened the port, stepped out into the thin, icy air. A cold wind chilled him. Among the plant-men a little wave of panic came. They shrank back. Mason lifted his hand, palm outward, in the immemorial gesture of peace.

Within his mind a wordless message stirred. "Who are you? You are not of the Deathless Ones?"

At a loss, Mason answered aloud. "We are friends. We seek food—"

Again the strange fear shook the creatures. They drew back further. One stood his ground, his blind glistening head turned toward the man, tentacles dangling limply.

"Food? What sort of food?"

They understood Mason's thoughts, apparently. Conscious that he was on dangerous ground, he said, "Anything you can spare. What you eat—"

"Who are you?"

"We come from the past," Mason answered at a venture. Would they understand that?

"You are not Deathless Ones?"

"No." Mason sensed that the Deathless Ones, whoever they were, were enemies of the plant-men. And his reply seemed to reassure the creatures.

They conferred, and again their spokesman stood forward. "We will give you food, what we can spare. We are the Gorichen." So Mason translated the plant-man's thought message. There was more confidence in the creature's mind now, he sensed.

"You must hurry, however. Soon the Wave will come..."

Puzzled, Mason nodded agreeably. "Bring what food you can spare, then."

"You must come with us. We may not carry food to the surface."

Mason considered, glanced back at the ship. "How far must I go?"

"Not far."

"Well, wait a minute." He went back to the others and explained what had happened. Murdach shook his head.

"I don't like it."

"They seem harmless enough. I'm not afraid of 'em. It's probably the other way around. They'll be glad to see the last of us. They're in deadly fear of some creatures they call the Deathless Ones, and they think we're related to them somehow."

"Well—" Murdach rubbed his lean jaw. "If you're not back soon, we'll come after you."

With a smile for Alasa, Mason leaped out through the port and approached the Gorichen. "I'm ready," he told them. "Let's get started."

Keeping a safe distance from the man, the plant-creatures led him to the edge of the great earth-crack. A sloping ladder led down into the depths. Several of them began to descend it swiftly, and more gingerly Mason followed.

It grew darker. A hundred feet down the ravine narrowed to a silt-covered floor, into which Mason's feet sank. The Gorichen led him toward a round metal disk, ten feet in diameter, that protruded from the ground. One of them fumbled at the disk with its pinkish tentacles. Silently metal slid aside, revealing a dim-lit hollow beneath.

Another ladder led down. At its bottom Mason found himself in a sloping corridor cut out of rock, leading into hazy distances. The plant-men urged him along this.

"How far?" Mason asked again.

"Soon, now."

But it was fully half an hour later when the Gorichen halted before a gleaming door at the end of the passage. It opened, and beyond it Mason saw a vast and shining cavern, hot with moist warmth. A musky, strong odor blew dankly against his face.

"We feed here," one of the Gorichen told Mason. "See?"

At a little distance was ranged a long row of flat, shallow basins set into the stone floor. Intense heat blazed down upon them. Within the basins was a black-scummed, oily liquid. As Mason watched a plant-man marched forward on his tentacles and lowered himself into a tank. He remained there unmoving.

"The rays from the great lamps overhead give us strength," a Gorichen told Mason with its thought-message. "Within the pits we have food, created artificially and dug out of our mines, dissolved in a liquor that aids the transmutation to chlorophyll."

The arrangement was logical enough, Mason realized. Plant-food, absorbed through the roots—radiation from the huge lights in the cavern's roof, a substitute for solar radiation, waning with the inevitable cooling of the Solar System. But such food was useless for human beings.

Mason said so. One of the Gorichen touched his arm with a soft tentacle-tip.

"It does not matter!

"What?" A chill premonition shook Mason. He glanced around swiftly at the blankly shining heads of the plant-men. "What d'you mean?"

"You are to be used in our experiments, that is all."

"Like Hell!" Mason snarled—and struck. His fist crashed out, pulping the body of one of the Gorichen. Its flesh was horribly soft and fungoid. Moist, soft stuff clung to Mason's hand. The Gorichen, a gaping hole in its torso, halted and then came forward again, apparently uninjured. And the others pressed toward the man, tentacles waving.

The battle was brief. Mason's muscles were toughened with fury and desperation, but he had no chance against overwhelming numbers. So at last he went down; was bound tightly, still struggling, with flexible metal ropes. Then the plant-men retreated, and Mason saw something that made his throat dry with horror.

A group of Gorichen were carrying a figure into the cavern—the body of Alasa, bound and silent, bronze hair hanging in disheveled ringlets about her pale face. She saw Mason. "Kent! They attacked us after you left! They killed Erech, I think. They—"

"Are you all right?" Mason asked, trying to regain his breath. "You're not hurt?"

She shook her head. "No. But Murdach escaped in the ship."

The Gorichen waited silently.

"Murdach escaped!" A little flare of hope mounted within Mason. Alasa seemed to read his thought.

"He can't help. We're under the ocean. These demons took me underground just as a great wave came out of the east..."

Now Mason realized why the plant-men dwelt underground. The Moon's nearness caused giant tides that swept resistlessly over the surface of the planet. Now they were far beneath the sea—and would be, until the tide retreated.

Mason grimaced. He tugged unavailingly at his bonds. One of the Gorichen came forward. His thought-message was clear. "We bear you no hatred. You say you are not of the Deathless Ones, our enemies. Yet you are very like them. For ages we have tried to find a way of defeating the Deathless Ones, and never yet have we succeeded. They cannot be captured. We cannot experiment on them. But you—if we find how you are vulnerable, we may use that knowledge on the Deathless Ones. Certain things we already know. Steel is useless. So are poisonous gases. But there are certain combinations of rays…"

The creature fell silent. His tentacles gestured, and the two captives were lifted, borne toward a glass block that towered near by. A door was opened in its side; Mason was thrust into its hollow interior. Cursing, he struggled with his bonds as the plant-men retreated with Alasa. Rolling over on his side, he peered though the transparent walls. And, watching, he went cold with horror.

To the Gorichen the two humans were guinea pigs, valuable only as material for their experiments. They dragged Alasa to an altar-like block of stone. Vainly she fought.

The tentacles of the monsters reached out, deftly removing the girl's clothing. In a moment she lay utterly nude, chained to the stone block so that she could scarcely move. A Gorichen wheeled a lens into position. From it a pale ray-beam fingered out, enveloping Alasa's ivory body in lambent moonglow.

She was unconscious, or seemed so. For a second the ray was visible; then it snapped out. Working hurriedly, the plant-men unbound the girl, carried her to Mason's prison, and thrust her within. They remained in little knots outside the glass walls, their blankly glistening heads inclined forward as though they stared attentively at the results of their experiment.

Cursing, Mason struggled to free himself. Useless attempt! The unyielding metal merely chafed and cut his wrists, and presently he stopped to glance at the girl. She was regaining consciousness.

She moaned, lifted a slim hand to brush bronze hair from her face. Slowly she opened her eyes. In them was a blind dreadful staring that made Mason catch his breath, his throat dry.

The girl dragged herself to her hands and knees. Her gaze moved questingly about the prison. She saw Mason.

Silently she crept forward. An angry flush was mounting in her face and bosom, and the glaring eyes grew wider.

"Alasa!" Mason called. *"Alasa!"*

No answer. The nude girl crawled toward him—and stopped. She arose.

Her breasts rose and fell more swiftly. A harsh cry came from her lips.

Then suddenly she sprang at him.

Mason was caught completely unawares. He could feel soft flesh pressed against his face, fever-hot, and caught a glimpse of Alasa's flashing teeth, bared in a distinct snarl. What kind of madness had the Gorichen's hellish ray worked?

Mason rolled away just in time as Alasa's teeth drove at his throat. Fingernails rued his face. Then Alasa leaped again, eyes blazing.

"God Almighty!" Mason groaned. Would he have to kill Alasa to escape being murdered? He drove the thought from his mind; he knew that he could never harm the girl even if she were insane. Yet, for her own sake, he must subdue her somehow. And he had little chance of doing that, bound as he was.

"Alasa!" he called again.

The girl did not heed.

Her body glistening with perspiration, she flung herself on Mason, fingers clawing, teeth seeking his throat. He tried to roll over, but could not.

A sharp pain lanced through his neck. He felt the warm stickiness of blood trickling across his skin.

Agonizingly the girl's teeth drove deeper...

CHAPTER EIGHT
The Deathless Ones

Dimly, through a red haze, Mason realized that the girl's weight no longer bore him down. Two plant-men held her writhing body in their tentacles, dragging her toward the door. A trickle of blood wormed from her lips. In silence she struggled, striving to break free.

The Gorichen pulled her outside. As Mason watched he saw her body suddenly sag limply in unconsciousness. A pang darted through him. Was Alasa—dead?

The same idea had come to the plant-men. Tentacles were waved excitedly. They lowered the girl to the floor, examining her carefully. A movement of Alasa's arm reassured Mason; the girl tried feebly to get to her feet.

The Gorichen dragged her back to Mason's prison. They thrust her within it. Again the door was shut.

Alasa ran to the man. "Kent! What happened?"

"You—" Mason hesitated. In the girl's eyes he read the knowledge that she remembered nothing of her nightmare attack on him. The madness of the plant-men had passed from her brain. "Nothing much," he flushed. "Can you untie me, Alasa?"

She bent forward, fumbled at the metal ropes. Would the Gorichen permit her to free the man?

At last the task was finished. Mason got to his feet, rubbing his legs to restore circulation. He went quickly to the door, kicked it tentatively.

The plant-men outside seemed to watch undisturbed.

Again Mason kicked the glass, but it did not shatter. He crashed his shoulder against it, but only bruised his arm. The cell was empty, and there was nothing he could use as a weapon.

A cry from Alasa made him turn. She was pointing to a corner of the cell, where walls joined ceiling. Greenish-white, a plume of vapor was entering the prison, coiling ominously in the still air.

Fear gripped Mason. He sprang forward, tried to reach the valve. If he could manage to stuff it closed—but it was too high. Baffled, he retreated to the door and renewed his onslaught on it.

But the substance, tougher than steel, would not yield. Mason paused only when he could scarcely see the door through a thickening cloud of greenish mist. Alasa touched his arm.

"Kent? What is happening?"

"I don't know," he said slowly. "They're experimenting on us. What they expect—well, I just don't know. Maybe it'll kill us. If it does, I hope it's a quick death."

With a soft little cry Alasa moved close to Mason, and he put protecting arms about her. She buried her face on his shoulder, and for a while they stood there, while the green mists thickened—thickened—

There came a time when Mason was completely blinded. Oddly he had no trouble with his breathing. There was a slight exhilaration, due, he thought, to oxygen in the strange gas, but he was not discommoded. Perhaps the vapor—admittedly experimental—would have no effect on human beings.

He dropped to the floor, cradling the girl in his arms. In that blind emerald emptiness they waited, and Mason soothed and calmed Alasa as best he could. In spite of himself his pulses mounted at the nearness of the girl's warm, satiny body. The weird gas, he knew, was exciting him; yet the madness grew on him. And Alasa, too, felt the intoxicating effect. Her hands crept up, touched Mason's hair. She drew down his head, guiding his lips in the green blindness till they touched her own. Flame of dark passion blazed up within Mason...

Desperately he fought it down. The girl's breathing mingled with his own, hoarse and uneven. His fingers touched the silken smoothness of rounded flesh, and the touch was like fire. Suddenly his muscles were weak as water.

"Alasa!" he whispered. *"Alasa!"*

In a surge of newfound strength he pressed the girl's form against him, sought her lips. Fantastic visions flashed through his mind. Weird madness of the plant-men's poisoned gas...

Alasa seemed to slide away, to vanish in a green-lit abyss. She was gone. Mason was alone. The clouds whirled about him, and very faintly he heard a distant throbbing, steadily growing louder. With the portion of his brain that remained sane he knew that this was unreal, a drug-born hallucination, as the deep pounding roared louder in his ears and dark shadows moved slowly down the emerald distance. Clearer the shadows grew, and clearer... Bat-winged horrors that mocked and tittered obscene laughter as they raced down on him...and ever the drumming roar grew deeper, louder, crashing like the tocsin of a demon in his ears...

Faster the green mist; swirled. They were a whirlwind of chaotic, blinding brilliance. The devils danced a grotesque saraband, screaming a mocking chant.

It swelled to a frightful crescendo of sound and motion that rocked Mason's giddy senses. He felt blackness creeping up and overwhelming him.

And it was with gratitude that he sank down into deepest unconsciousness!

Slowly Mason awoke, with a blinding headache and an acrid, unpleasant taste in his mouth. He opened his eyes, stared up at the transparent roof of his prison. He was still imprisoned in the crystal cage, but the green gas had been pumped out. Alasa's still body lay beside him. Head swimming. Mason tried to revive her. He stripped off his cloak and wrapped it about the girl.

A grating overhead made him look up. The roof of the cage was sliding aside, leaving a gap four feet wide, running the length of the prison. Plant-men were busy with a kind of crane, swinging its burden, an enigmatic metal block, into place so that it could be dropped into the two human's prison. There came an interruption.

The Gorichen sprang into frenzied activity. Mason could not interpret their thoughts, but he sensed sudden, deadly danger. Frantically the plant-men went racing toward the corridor that led into the upper world. A stray thought-fragment flashed into Mason's mind.

"The Deathless Ones! They have broken the gateway—"

In five minutes the cavern was deserted. Now, if ever, was a chance to escape. Mason looked up once more. The smooth sides of the cell were unscalable. But above the gap in the roof hung the metallic block from the crane's arm, too high to be reached—unless—

A rope? Mason wore only the loincloth Erech had given him in Al Bekr, and neither that nor the cloak would support his weight. His glance fell on the metal ropes that had bound him, now discarded in a mound on the floor, and Mason knew he had solved the problem. If only they were long enough!

Picking them up, he paused to examine Alasa. Already assured of her safety, it was with relief that he saw the girl's lashes flutter, and her golden eyes open. She saw Mason.

"Oh, Kent! Help me up!" She clutched his arm, got unsteadily to her feet. "We're not dead, it seems. I thought we were both slain and in the Pit of Abaddon—"

"Maybe you're right about the last," Mason said grimly. He told her what had happened. "If I can loop the rope over that metal block, we can climb out, I think."

"Can you do it?"

He shook his head doubtfully. "I can try…"

But only after repeated attempts did Mason manage to loop the doubled end of the metal cord over the suspended block. Then a careless move undid his work, and for another ten minutes he tried, a fury of apprehension mounting within him, till at last the anxious work was done. The two ends of the rope hung down within the cell. Mason knotted them together.

"I'll go first. Then I'll pull you up—"

The metal cord was slippery, scoring Mason's skin. He twisted his legs about it, fought his way up, while Alasa held the rope steady from below. And at last he reached the roof of the cell, swung on to it, sweating with exertion.

"Hurry!" he told the girl. Distant sounds of conflict made him fear that the cavern would not be isolated for long.

His muscles, weary with exertion and lack of food, cracked and strained as he hauled Alasa painfully to his side. But it was easier thereafter. They slid down to the floor of the cavern, and swiftly made for the passage that led to freedom.

"It's the only way out, apparently," Mason said, glancing around. "Hold on! There's something I want."

He retrieved a bar of silvery metal, longer than his arm, that would made a formidable bludgeon. He tested it with a vicious swing that smashed the crytic gears of a machine.

"Good! It isn't soft or brittle. This'll help, Alasa!"

The girl responded by picking up a smaller bar for herself. Battle-light glowed in her golden eyes. She hurried at Mason's side, the cloak occasionally flaring to reveal the pale flesh of her thighs.

But before they reached the passage-mouth a battling horde spewed from it, struggling in insane conflict. Swiftly Mason caught the girl, drew her down out of sight. Crouching, they watched.

The Gorichen were fighting for their lives. And their enemies were...

The Deathless Ones! Icy cold crawled down Mason's back as he saw the invaders, creatures that were unmistakably human beings, yet more alien to him than the grotesque plant-men. For the Gorichen were normal products of evolution, and the Deathless Ones, Mason sensed, were not.

They were the living dead. In their bodies dwelt life-undying, forms that had once been tall and stalwart and god-like in their beauty. Even now some remnant of past splendor lingered, made dreadful by the foul corruption that had overtaken the Deathless Ones.

The name itself explained much. They were men who had conquered death—but not disease! Not—corruption!

All the hideous plagues of mankind had burst into foul ripening on the bodies of the Deathless Ones. None was whole. Loathsome gaping wounds and sores showed the flesh and bone beneath. Tatters of granulated flesh hung in ribbons from some. There were unspeakable skull-faces glaring blindly, and there were mutilations from which Mason turned away, sickened.

Man had conquered death—and, too late, had discovered his error.

The Deathless Ones seemingly could not be injured. Scores of the Gorichen would leap upon an enemy, bearing him down by their weight. And presently the pile of struggling figures would fall away, and show that at the bottom the Deathless One had been busy—feeding.

Mason remembered he had seen no plant or animal life on the surface of the planet. Possibly the Gorichen were the only food of the Deathless One...

The struggle swept away from the tunnel-mouth. With a whispered command Mason gripped Alasa's arm, sprang out from concealment. They heard a dreadful cry go up, heard feet thudding in pursuit. A hand closed on Mason's arm; he whirled; struck out blindly with his weapon, felt unclean flesh pulp under the blow. The grip fell away and was gone.

The two humans fled up the passage, black fear pacing them.

Were there more of the monsters in the tunnel? Mason gripped the metal bar tighter at the thought. The sounds of pursuit grew fainter, but did not die away.

Slowly the couple's speed grew less. Their hearts were throbbing painfully; their throats parched and dry. An increasing tumult from below made them increase their pace. But they could not keep it up. Once more the Deathless Ones gained.

Alasa stumbled, almost fell. Mason dragged her upright, ran on supporting her with his arm about her waist. "We ought to be near the surface now," he told the girl, and she looked up with a quick smile.

"Soon, now, Kent..."

The pursuers came faster. Mason caught sight of a gleam of silvery daylight lancing down from overhead. The door to the outer Earth!

They reached the ladder, climbed it with frantic haste, the clamoring monsters almost within arm's length. In the ravine Mason pointed up.

"The ladder, Alasa. I'll hold 'em back and then come after you."

She hesitated, and then obeyed. Mason's inattention was almost his undoing. A talon-like hand seized his foot, almost overbalancing him. A frightful skull-face rose out of the pit, screaming with wordless, dreadful hunger. Mason sent the metal bar smashing down, sick revulsion clawing at his stomach.

Bone and brain shattered under the blow. Blindly the thing tried to crawl up, though its head was a pulped, gory horror. The mouth of the pit was choked with dozens of the Deathless Ones, greedy for flesh to feed their avid maws, heedless of blows, pushing up and up...

Mason battered them down, till the very weight of the monsters bore them in a tangled heap to fall back into the passage. Then, gripping the bar in one hand, he ran swiftly up the ladder and rejoined Alasa on the surface.

"I've an idea," he said, grinning feebly, swaying on his feet. "Those things can't be very intelligent. The plant-men are, but—"

Mason stooped, pulled up the ladder. A group of Deathless Ones emerged from the pit, roaring menace. Spying Mason, they tried to climb the walls of the ravine, but failed. Presently a few of them set off to right and left.

"There may be another way out. We'd better scram—depart, I mean," Mason said at Alasa's puzzled look. "Come on."

"But—where?"

The man scanned the dark sky. A wan Sun glowed huge and red. The Moon had vanished. A chill wind blew over a plain of wet, featureless silt.

"I don't know. Away from the coast, anyway. If we can find Murdach and the ship..."

Silently they set out, trudging across the lonely waste, shuddering in the icy wind that rushed bleakly over the surface of a dying planet.

CHAPTER NINE
Tower of the Mirage

For hours the two struggled through the sticky ooze, up the slope of a slowly rising plain. In the thin air their lungs pumped painfully. Twice Mason saw something flying overhead, vague in the distance, but he could not make out its nature. It was apparently winged, and was clearly not the time-ship.

But they found the ship at last, almost by chance. Its silvery surface glowed like a flame in the gray, dull plain. It seemed hours before they reached it.

And it was empty. Murdach and Erech had vanished. There were signs of struggle, and a pool of dried blood on the floor. In the mud outside a confused track led toward the east. Frowning, Mason swung shut the door and turned to the controls.

"I can move the ship, Alasa. Maybe we can find Erech and Murdach. That spoor's pretty clear."

The girl wrapped her cloak more closely about her slender body. "Do so, Kent." She found a flask of water and offered it to Mason before she drank.

Slowly the craft rose, drifted on above the waste, following the track. On the horizon a spire rose, growing taller as they advanced. It was a cyclopean crag—not the work of nature. It was too regular, Mason realized, a great cylindrical shaft that thrust itself from the gray empty plain into the gray sky, flat-topped, desolate and colossal.

"They may be in that," Mason suggested. "See if you can find some weapons, Alasa."

Presently the girl gave him Murdoch's egg-shaped projector. "It worked on the metal men," she told him. "Whether it will succeed in killing living beings I do not know."

"Well, it's better than nothing. I still have my club." Mason glanced down at the metal bar.

The surface of the tower was, perhaps, two miles across, and quite flat. There was an odd flickering in the air above it, and once or twice Mason caught a fugitive glimpse of bright color that flashed out from the gray desolation of the tower and was gone. In the exact center was a round, black opening, and toward this Mason lowered the ship slowly.

He landed on the rim—almost losing control of the craft in his surprise. For directly beneath him, springing out of empty nothingness, loomed a great granite boulder! It was twenty feet high, and he was slanting toward it, paralyzed with astonishment and horror. With a grating crash the ship landed.

The shock almost threw him from his feet. The boulder—was gone! He followed the direction of Alasa's astonished gaze, turned and saw the boulder behind the ship. Apparently they had passed through it as though it were a phantom.

Nor was this all. All around, where he had seen nothing but a flat, metallic surface from the air, was a wilderness of tumbled, riven rock. To all sides towered the great boulders, and overhead a blazing *white* sun glared down.

"Good lord!" Mason grasped. "We haven't move in time! What's happened?"

"Magic," Alasa said, solving the problem to her own satisfaction. "Do you think Erech and Murdach are here?"

"If they are, they flew in." As Mason spoke he realized his guess was not too far-fetched. He had seen creatures flying in the air—perhaps the very beings that had captured the vanished pair.

"I hope Erech is not dead," the girl murmured. "Shall we search, Kent?"

Nodding, Mason opened the port, stepped out, followed by the girl. He approached the great rock and tried to touch it. His hand passed through the brown, rugose surface as though it did not exist.

"It's a mirage," Mason said suddenly, with conviction. "An unbelievably perfect one! Three-dimensional! Artificially created, I'm sure. Look at your feet, Alasa."

The girl's slim ankles were hidden, seemingly, in gray, slate-like rock. But she stepped forward without hindrance. Mason moved to her side, felt the smooth surface of the flat tower top beneath him. He got down and felt the cold metal with his hands. Then, smiling a little, he plunged first his hand and then his head into one of the great phantom boulders, and found himself instantly in profound darkness. He heard Alasa cry out.

He moved back, and there was the white sun pouring down its non-existent, heatless rays, and all around was the tumbled wilderness of jagged rock.

"Your head," the girl said shakily. "It—vanished!"

"Yeah," Mason nodded. "And I've just thought of something. That hole in the roof. We'd better be careful, or we'll both vanish for good. There may be a stairway going down it, though."

Trying to remember the location of the gap, he stepped forward cautiously, gripping the girl's hand. They waded through intangible rocks that sometimes came up to their waist. It was fantastic, incredible science of an alien world.

And suddenly Mason felt a mighty throbbing that grew and pulsed all about him. The wilderness of barren rock trembled and shivered, like a painted curtain rustling in the wind, and abruptly it—changed! Like a motion-picture fading from one scene to another the panorama of rocks that seemed to stretch to the horizon grew vague and disappeared, and in its place grew another scene, a weird, alien landscape that hemmed in the pair as though they had been transported to another world.

All about them now was a tangled forest of luxuriant vegetation, and the bark of the trees, as well as the leaves, the thick masses of vines, even the grass underfoot was an angry brilliant crimson. Nor was that the worst. The things were alive!

The vines writhed and swung on the trees, and the trees themselves swayed restlessly, their branches twisting in the air. No wind stirred them. They were living beings, and even the long, curiously serpentine red grass at their feet made nauseating little worm-motions.

There was no Sun—just an empty blue sky, incongruously beautiful and peaceful amid the writhing horrors that hemmed them in, the forest that was as immaterial as the phantom rocks had been.

"Wait a minute," Mason said. He took a few steps back, for a curious theory was forming in his mind. And again came the mighty throbbing and the strange crawling and shifting of the red forest, and as he retreated it melted swiftly into the familiar wilderness of jagged rock. Alasa had vanished. Looking over his shoulder, Mason could see the time-ship beside the great boulder. He moved forward again and Alasa sprang into view, her golden eyes wide and frightened.

"Okay," he told her. "Let's hunt for the hole, eh?"

"Here it is, Kent. I almost fell into it." She pointed at the wormy tangle of red grass nearby. Mason stared. Of course, he could not see down into the gap. The scarlet vegetation hid it. He knelt and, overcoming his repugnance, thrust his face down through the twisting grasses. He was in empty blackness—below the ground level in the world of the red plants, Mason knew.

A curious conviction came to the man that these scenes, the strange mirages on the tower, were not merely created phantoms, but actual reflections of real worlds that exist, or did exist, or will exist in the future. He circled cautiously about the gap.

It was about twenty feet across. His fumbling hands found an incline going down into the darkness, slippery and too steep to walk upon. It went down at an angle of about forty-five degrees, as well as Mason could judge, crawling on his hands and knees and feeling there in the empty darkness.

"Kent," the girl said with quiet urgency. "Listen!"

"Eh? What—"

Then he heard it—a harsh, very loud scratching noise. It came from the depths of the invisible shaft. It grew louder, and a sudden premonition made Mason seize Alasa's hand and retreat swiftly. It was lucky that he did.

The thing came out of the shaft, and first they saw a bristle of waving antennae, and two huge claws jerking convulsively in empty air. It came rising inexorably out of the ground, and in a moment they saw the whole frightful being.

"An ant!" Mason heard himself whispering. "A winged ant!"

But it was a colossus. Twenty-five feet long it towered, mandibles clashing, wings outspread, rustling dryly as they clashed against the wing-cases, crawling up blindly.

The creature moved forward. It was blind, Mason guessed. No eyes were visible, but the antennae apparently took their place. The claws clicked menacingly.

Horror turned Mason cold. As the thing advanced he flung himself back, pulling Alasa with him.

"The ship!" he said unsteadily. "Come!"

The white-faced girl nodded and kept pace with him. At a venture Mason raced in the direction he thought the ship lay. His guess was wrong.

Almost immediately he heard the throbbing and saw the wavering and shifting, and then they were rushing through— nothingness! Empty fog, gray billows of thick stuff that were so turbid he was completely blinded. Thinking with lightning speed, Mason turned at right angles, dragging Alasa, and cut across in a frantic attempt to locate the ship.

He heard a clashing, a dry rustling—the giant ant, hurrying in pursuit. Madness of fear tugged at Mason's brain. It was the quintessence of horror, wading through rocks he could not feel, racing through trees that did not exist. The ant trailed its prey by scent, or by some less familiar sense, and as it was blind, the shifting three-dimensional mirages made no difference to it. They had been created, apparently, to confuse the enemies of the ant-monsters.

Mason and Alasa would be sprinting through what seemed to be a field of emeralds, glinting under a hazy sky with a low-hanging moon, when there would come the shifting and throbbing, and the panorama would fade away like the mirage it was. And in its place would come, perhaps, a vast field of frozen white, with not an object visible and a black, starless sky overhead. Once they were hurrying through a green swirl of water, with seaweed drifting by and curious creatures swimming past them—through them! A thing like a great opaque white ball, pulsating and writhing, drifted at Mason, and he leaped aside, shuddering.

Then they would hear the dry rustling, and it would be bolt, sprint, race with temples throbbing and sweat running into their eyes, till the two would be forced to fling themselves down and rest while they gasped for breath. They went zigzagging and plunging through a weird and fantastic array of alien worlds and scenes. Mason could not help flinching when a great tree or wall of ice would loom in his path, though he knew the thing was an impalpable phantom.

Then, too, there was the ever-present fear that they would plunge off the edge of the tower. What saved them was nearly their doom, for as they went racing through a curiously regular rank of thin columns, like bamboo, that stretched up to a far whiteness that was either the sky or an incredibly lofty roof, they burst suddenly into the world of living vegetation. Mason went rushing through a swaying red tree. The rasping sound of pursuit was loud in his ears—and his feet went from under him.

Letting go of Alasa's hand, he fell heavily on his side, sliding down till his hips were on the polished slide that led down into the interior of the tower and the lair of the ant-monster. He kept on sliding.

Desperately, Mason gave a frantic twist and squirm that nearly broke his back; he felt Alasa's hands pulling him to safety. The girl's white body gleamed through the flaring cloak. Somehow, Mason scrambled to his feet, his breath a flaming agony within his lungs.

The monster was nearly on them. Remembering Murdach's weapon, Mason clawed it out, aimed it. A thin beam sprang at the giant ant. Light crawled weirdly over the frightful head.

And the thing—died! Without a sound it dropped, though its impetus carried it forward till it slid over the brink of the abyss and vanished from light. No sound came from below.

Trembling a little, Mason replaced the weapon. "Come on, Alasa," he said shakily. "We've got to find the ship. There may be more of those devils around."

But it was not easy to locate the vessel. The two played a weird game of blind-man's-bluff there on the top of the tower, hurrying through mirages, some they recognized, others totally unfamiliar. Some were horrible and others pleasant enough.

The worst was hurrying over a black, gelatinous substance that heaved restlessly underfoot, like the hide of some Cyclopean monster, and it might have been, for all he knew. The black, heaving skin seemed to stretch for miles around, and sometimes the two were buried to their hips in it.

Again they were hurrying across a field of hard, frozen brown earth, with a phenomenally beautiful night sky overhead, studded with constellations and gleaming planets, entirely unfamiliar. A great comet glowed in its white glory among the stars. Then there was a surface of ice or glass, and looking down Mason could see, far below, vague and indistinct figures that seemed entirely inhuman, as far as he could make out through the cloudy crystalline substance.

They staggered through a world of blazing fire, flinching as heatless tongues of flame licked at them. They reeled across a vast desert of sand that crawled and billowed beneath them, stirring with a monstrous embryonic life.

But at last they found the ship. With heartfelt relief Mason followed Alasa aboard and closed the door, sent the vessel lancing up. The girl sank down in a limp heap, her breasts heaving tumultuously.

At a safe distance above the tower Mason stopped the ship, hovering there, while he pondered. Were Erech and Murdach captive within the huge eidolon? Or...

A cry from Alasa made him turn. She was pointing. "Look! It's—"

"Erech!" Mason finished excitedly. "And Murdach!"

Crawling across the gray plain, almost at the foot of the tower now, was one of the giant ants, carrying in its claws two limp figures that were, even at the distance, unmistakably human. His hand closing on the weapon in his pocket, Mason sent the ship flashing down.

But—the thought came—could he use the ray projector on the monster without killing his friends? No, he couldn't risk it.

The huge ant seemed to sense danger. It paused, antenna questing, as the ship dropped toward it. Then, dropping its burdens, it spread its wings and mounted to do battle!

CHAPTER TEN
The People of the Pyramid

Grimly Mason guided the ship forward. The tensile strength of the craft he did not know, but he suspected that under the ant's chitinous armor it was fragile. In this he was wrong.

A blow of the monster's wing crashed against the ship, sent it whirling, hurling Mason and Alasa from their feet. He caught a glimpse of the tower rushing toward him, managed to drag himself upright against the controls. With scarcely a foot to spare the vessel looped around and went driving back toward the winged colossus.

The creature came to meet them. In the last moment before impact Mason's fingers stabbed at the panel, attempting to change course. But he was too late. With a grinding, frightful impact, the winged monster and time-ship came together—catastrophically.

Mason was hurled back, his fingers raking blindly over the control keys. He had a flashing vision of the ant's shattered body plummeting to the plain below, and then intense blackness was all around him. Something thudded against his head, and in his last second of consciousness Mason realized what the darkness meant. The ship, unguided, was racing through time!

Only for a moment, it seemed, was Mason out. Groaning with pain in his throbbing head, he lifted himself to his feet and fumbled blindly in the darkness for the controls. Then, suddenly, he realized that the gloom was not complete. Through the ship's transparent walls he saw a star-bright sky above, and an uneven black wall around, apparently a rampart of trees. The ship lay tilted perilously on its side. He saw a pale blotch in a corner, Alasa's face.

He could not aid her while she lay on the sharply slanting floor. Mason opened the port, managed to scramble out, half-carrying Alasa. Underfoot was a layer of humus, half-rotted vegetation with a clank, musky odor. The air was uncomfortably hot and moist.

Fumbling in the starlight, Mason tried to revive the girl.

She sat up eventually, clinging to him, rubbing a bruise on her shoulder.

"That ant—where are we, Kent? Did we find Erech and Murdach?"

"I guess not," Mason told her. "Apparently the time-controls were accidentally moved when we hit the giant ant. We've probably come through time to this sector, and crashed while we were unconscious. It's sheer luck that we didn't have our necks broken. I guess the ground surface is higher here than in the future time—that may account for it."

"But where are we?"

"I haven't the slightest idea. I don't think we went forward—this thick forest, and the heat, indicates a past era. I hope it isn't the Cretaceous. I'd hate to meet a tyrannosaur."

"What's that?" the girl asked, her eyes wide.

"A—a dragon. The name means thunder lizard. But—"

And then the attack came. Mason had heard no noise in the underbrush. But out of the forest dark figures came charging. There was no warning. Before Mason had a chance to brace himself he went down, a dozen wiry bodies swarming over him—and then fire burst in the back of his head. Red fire that was swallowed up by abysmal blackness...

He awoke in the dimness of what seemed to be a crudely-built hut. Warm sunlight slanted through the doorway; a human shadow—shadow of a guard—darkened the floor. Mason shook his head, groaning. He heard a low, muffled chanting.

And—recognized it! In his archeological work, probing into the far corners of the globe, Mason had acquired a sound knowledge of little-known dialects. He had heard similar sounds, long ago, floating down a South American river in a hollow log dugout, his arm throbbing and festering with the wound of an arrow.

Had he, by some incredible chance, returned to his own time-sector?

The doorway darkened. Men filed in, nearly naked little men, with brown, muscular bodies. They were grotesquely painted, and feathers nodded and waved in their hair. Chanting, they freed Mason's legs. Leathern thongs, he realized, still bound his wrists.

Hesitatingly Mason spoke, trying to remember that alien dialect of years ago.

"I am—a friend—"

A native struck his mouth. "Silence!" The word was oddly accented, but recognizable. "You are to watch, not to speak." Again the chant rose.

"Hear our prayers, O Thunderer! Hear the prayers of the Curupuri—"

The natives urged him outside the hut. Mason blinked, accustoming his eyes to the strong sunlight. He stared around.

The towering walls of a crater marched on the horizon. Black basalt ramparts hemmed them in. To the east was a jagged gap, apparently a pass. At their feet the ground sloped down to the motionless, sullen waters of a lake.

No wind ruffled its surface. Dark, enigmatic, it filled the crater, save for the narrow strip of land on which the native village stood. The score of flimsy huts were in curious contrast to the stone pyramid that stood on the lake's shore.

Mason was pushed toward it. Its shadow fell on him. It was perhaps thirty feet high, built of huge blocks of stone, without mortar. In one side was a gaping aperture. Into this the white man was conducted.

A short passage, and then a room, half underground—a temple, Mason realized. Amazement lanced through him. At one end of the chamber was a raised dais, on which stood a chair—a throne, gleaming dully in the light of torches. A golden throne, jewel studded!

Its build was suggestive of Incan workmanship. Yet these brown-skinned natives were not Incas. Perhaps Incas had built this pyramid, and had been killed by the invading tribe—the Curupuri, as they called themselves, Mason hazarded.

This was the past, he knew. A time perhaps long before Columbus had reached the Indies, certainly prior to the coming of the Spanish Conquistadores.

On the throne a corpse sat. A mummy, withered and shrunken and dry, in whose eye-sockets glowed two flaming rubies. Golden breastplates and a girdle of gold hung loosely on the skeletal figure.

Beside the throne stood a native girl, her amber body scarcely hidden by a translucent feathery cape, through which alluring curves were visible. Her sullen eyes brooded on the white man.

On the walls were heads. Smaller than coconuts, shrunken by some secret process that preserved flesh and features, their multitude almost hid the rough stones. Natives' heads, all of them.

The chanting grew louder. A dozen gaudily-painted Curupuri filed into the chamber. Among them was Alasa. For a moment her golden eyes met Mason's.

"Kent!" she cried. "They—"

A guard clapped a rough hand over her mouth. Cursing, Mason wrenched at his bonds. His captors held him, silent and impassive.

The Curupuri took the girl up to the dais, clamped golden rings about her ankles. From the throng a dwarfish native stepped to stand beside the girl. His face was hideous with paint. From a bald, shaved head white feathers nodded, set in a jewel-studded headdress. The man lifted his hand, and the noise quieted.

From the Curupuri came a great shout.

"Zol!"

The native girl stepped forward. Mason read hatred in her eyes as she glanced at the dwarfish Zol.

Again came the deep-throated roar.

"Yana! Ho—Yana!"

Zol threw back his head, the white feathers bowing. He cried, "The Thunderer looks with favor upon us."

He pointed to the withered corpse on the throne.

"For years she has sat there, ruling the Curupuri in death. Since she lived we have found no girl with a skin white enough to be our priestess. So Yana has served—"

He glanced slyly at the priestess beside him.

"But now her toil has ended. From the skies has fallen a maiden with a skin white as foam. Almost we slew her—but the Thunderer stayed my stroke."

From the Curupuri came a roaring chant.

"Ho! Dweller in the Abyss. Dark Thunderer—hear us!"

The girl Yana cried, "Hear our prayers! Drink—eat of our sacrifice!" Her red lips were cruel.

"Lord of the Lake!" thundered the Curupuri. "Look on our sacrifice!"

Then silence, heavy and ominous. Yana said, "The priestess must be unblemished." Her voice was sweetly malicious.

Zol nodded, turned to Alasa. His hands went out, ripping the tattered cloak from her. A gasp went up from the natives.

The girl stood nude. Her bronze hair spilled in a tumbled mass on bare shoulders. Instinctively her hands went up in an attempt to cover herself.

Zol shouted laughter as he gazed at the nude girl, at the sweeping curves of her body, flawless in its beauty. Then the priest tore the feather cloak from Yana and cast it about Alasa's shoulders.

Nausea tore at Mason's throat as he saw the body of the priestess naked save for a brief loincloth. From neck to ankles she had been tattooed. Red and blue designs circled the mounds of her breasts, fled across her rounded hips. Understanding the months of agony the girl must have endured made Mason feel suddenly sick.

The shouting died. Zol chanted, "She is unmarred— perfect! Tonight the testing begins. The mark of the Thunderer shall be put upon her."

The mark of Thunderer? Alasa shuddered, drew the translucent cloak closer. In the eyes of Yana, Mason saw a red blaze of rage. Her lashes drooped, she turned away.

The Curupuri closed about Mason. Vainly struggling, he was forced from the temple, taken back to the hut. There, legs once more bound, he was left alone.

The afternoon dragged on. Occasionally the guard would enter to test the captive's bonds. Though Mason tried to engage in conversation with the man, he met with no success. Perhaps the Curupuri were forbidden to converse with their prisoners.

Just after sunset Mason heard voices outside the hut, and presently Yana, the priestess, entered. Two natives were at her heels.

One was the guard. He freed Mason's feet, and with the other Curupuri, left the hut. The priestess knelt beside Mason.

In the dimness the disfiguring tattooing was invisible, and Mason could see only the smooth curves of the girl's body, scarcely hidden by thin cloth. She said softly, "The guard is gone. I told him Zol wished him to hunt in the forest. And the other who waits without—is my friend."

Mason stared at her. Fumbling with the Curupuri dialect, he said, "One has need of friends here."

She nodded. "It is true. I—would like to save the white girl?"

"Yes!" Mason said swiftly. "Will you help me?"

"Perhaps."

"Why?" He did not entirely trust this girl in whose eyes murderous rage sprang so easily.

"In your place I should not hesitate. You are strangers, I know that. You are not gods, as some said, else you would not be bound and helpless now. Whence you come I do not care, so long as you leave here swiftly."

"The—the place where we were captured. Is it far from here?"

"No. You saw the gap in the mountains—the pass? It is not far, just beyond that. You can reach it in a fourth part of a day. And as for why I shall help you—it is because the white girl will take my place! For years a pale-skinned priestess of our tribe has ruled us. When the last one died I took her place. Zol did not like that—for I would not always obey him. Now he sees a chance to depose me and gain a puppet priestess. I would kill this white girl, but it would be sacrilege. I would be tortured…but if you escape with her, it will be different."

"Then untie me," Mason said, his voice eager.

The girl bent down, her hair brushing Mason's face. "But you must not fail! For there is another way—" Again the mad rage flared in her eyes. "I have been the priestess of the Thunderer for more than a year. And I have learned much— the words of power that call the Dark Lord from the lake." Her tone was brooding. "I had it in mind to use those words. Once before it was done, ages ago, and the Dweller rose from the depths. The Curupuri died—all but a few, who fled."

She shrugged, and her knife flashed, slicing through the last thongs that bound Mason. He stretched cramped muscles. "Tell me," he said curiously, "have you ever seen any white men not of your tribe? Like me?"

"No. Never. I did not think any existed. Our priestesses had golden skin, not as white as yours," She watched Mason speculatively. "You must wait. It will be dark soon. If you leave the hut now you will be killed."

The hard anger was gone from Yana's eyes; they were strangely tender. "You are not like the Curupuri. And— since I became a priestess—I have not known…love…"

Suddenly her arms were about Mason's neck, her breath hot against his cheek as she strained against him. Mad torrents of passion seemed unleashed in the priestess. She whispered softly, "I have not known love. And—"

Mason tried to free himself. The girl drew back, her face hardening. She said, "No? Remember—you have not freed the white girl yet. If I should summon aid—"

Mason grinned wryly. Then Yana was in his arms once more. It was not easy to resist—no! Under the thin cloth of her garment he felt the alluring curves of her body.

Shrugging, Mason bent his head, touched the girl's lips. He did not draw back. The moist inferno of her mouth quickened his pulses. Within the priestess was the hot soul of flame, breath of the searing *Zonda* that blows across the pampas—hungry passion that surged through Mason like a rushing tide.

She shuddered, moaned. A noise came from outside the hut. Instantly Yana pulled away, a finger at her lips.

"Wait…"

She disappeared outside. Mason heard her voice raised in dispute with a deeper one; then the two died slowly in the distance. He crept to the entrance, peered out. No one was visible nearby, though a few Curupuri moved aimlessly about the village in the distance. The sun was already low.

He would not have to wait long.

Two hours later it was dark enough to make the venture. The guard had not returned. He slunk out of his prison. The moon had just risen, and he kept in the shadows of the huts. A heavy club discarded by a dying fire caught his eye, and he confiscated it.

He moved toward the pyramid, a muffled chanting waking ominous apprehensions within him. He caught a glimpse of motion on the summit, and he thought he saw Alasa's bronze hair, though he could not be sure.

Glancing aside at the lake, Mason involuntarily shuddered. What had Yana said? A Thunderer in the depths—a monster-god to whom the Curupuri sacrificed. In this dawn of history, could some strange survival actually exist beneath those sullen waters? Even in his day there had been legends of the South American swamps and jungles…

CHAPTER ELEVEN
Blood on the Pyramid

Mason halted near the base of the pyramid. On the structure's flat top gleamed a golden throne, and on it was the mummified corpse of the former priestess. In the moonlight Mason saw Zol, the squat priest, standing there, and beside him a group of other natives.

And Alasa was there, wearing the feather robe, in the grip of two natives. The low chant grew louder. Abruptly Zol turned, removed the breastplate and girdle from the corpse, and lifted the mummy from the throne. He swung the body thrice around his head—then sent it arcing down till the black waters of the lake broke in a silvery spray.

The mummy floated briefly; then there was a brief commotion, and the thing was dragged down. It vanished. The chanting swelled to a triumphant roar.

Mason moved forward cautiously, the cudgel in his hand, as Zol lifted the feather cape from Alasa's bare shoulders. She stood nude in the moonlight, a glorious statue of loveliness. Vainly she struggled as she was dragged to the throne, seated within it, her arms and legs bound securely. Zol beckoned, and a Curupuri came forward, a deep bowl in his hands.

Others advanced, bearing a long pole to which a native was bound. A great shout thundered out.

From the shadows men came—the Curupuri tribe, thronging about the base of the pyramid, watching the drama being enacted on its summit. Mason drew back, his fingers whitening on the club.

Zol's hand moved swiftly, a blade flashed, and a bubbling scream of agony came from the captive. Blood fountained from his throat. Deftly the priest thrust the bowl beneath the gaping wound, filled the vessel.

The men on the pyramid were silent—waiting. Zol dipped his hands into the bowl, lifted them dripping red. He smeared the blood on Alasa's nude body, till from neck to ankles her slender form gleamed crimson. He lifted the knife again, lowered it gently. Its point touched Alasa's bare stomach.

The girl cried out sharply. This, Mason guessed, was the beginning of the tattooing ceremony. For months thereafter Alasa would endure the frightful torture of sharp knives, of agonizing pain of pigments rubbed into the raw wounds till her body was covered, like the priestess', with fantastic designs.

Again the knife came down. Again Alasa cried out—a soft, frightened cry that sent red madness surging into Mason's brain.

He lifted the cudgel as he sprang forward. A line of natives barred him from the pyramid, but he broke through the Curupuri with a murderous sweep of his weapon that sent a man sprawling head smashed into pulp. Shouting, Mason sprinted forward.

Behind him he heard a deep-throated roar. He ignored it, racing up the rough stones of the pyramid that offered easy foothold. On the summit men were milling about, staring down, their weapons drawn. Before they could organize he was among them.

He saw a snarling face, pale in the moonlight, looming up before him—and swung the club. The man went down, screaming.

"Take him!" Zol shouted. "Take him—alive!"

Then suddenly the priest was racing forward, a spear in his hand, arm drawn back for the throw. Mason sent the cudgel spinning at his opponent.

His aim was true. The missile crashed into Zol's face, obliterating the brown features in a smear of blood. Red spurted from the man's flattened nose. Screaming, he went down.

But already a dozen Curupuri were on Mason; grimly he slugged and kicked and clawed. A bare foot kicked viciously at his face. He twisted his head away in time to avoid the blow.

But Mason went down at last, fighting desperately. He felt his hands being drawn behind him, saw Alasa straining forward on the throne, her body darkly crimson. She cried, "Kent, are you hurt? Did they—"

"I'm okay," he said—and Zol came forward, his ruined face bloody and hideous. He glared down at the white man.

"Soon you will die." His whisper was fury-soft. "But not slowly—no!"

He turned to the lake, lifted the sacrificial knife.

"Dweller in the Abyss," he chanted. "The priestess is prepared. Soon she will serve you."

Mason strained to escape from the arms that held him. Useless!

The Curupuri below the pyramid roared applause at the priest.

Then silence. And cutting through it a thin, high scream that made the short hairs prickle on Mason's neck. There was defiance in that scream—desperate rage, and horror, and something above and beyond all these. The priest hesitated, looked down. His jaw dropped.

Mason turned his head. On the beach, knee-deep in the black waters, was Yana the priestess, nude, a golden statue in the moonlight. Her black hair streamed in the wind. She lifted her arms; her red lips parted. From them came again that dreadful cry...

"Alien, Summoning!"

Summoning—*what?*

The priest shrilled, "Slay her! Slay her!"

The others streamed down from the pyramid's summit, racing toward Yana, save for two who still held Mason motionless. The priestess cried again that strange call.

In Zol's face Mason read something that made him look out across the lake. A few ripples troubled the black surface. That was all.

No...there was more.

Something was moving toward the shore, a dark and tremendous bulk that glided through the waters with unhurried smoothness. Something that could never exist in a sane world...

And now Mason remembered Yana's words: "I have learned much—the words of power that call the Thunderer from the lake. Once before it was done, ages ago, and the Dweller rose from the depths..."

The god of the Curupuri had answered the summoning of his priestess. Through the dark inky waters the thing glided, and a black, shining bulk arose in the moonlight, a flat and serpentine head and a long, undulating column of neck...

Zol's face was a Gorgon mask of horror abysmal. The natives were almost at the lake's shore—and they shrank back. Yana screamed her weird call—and the cry turned into a shriek as the monster was upon her.

The giant head swooped, lifted with the girl's body dangling from immense jaws. Cold, reptilian eyes surveyed the village. As the girl vanished into the thing's maw the creature lumbered up onto the beach.

Desperately Mason tried to rationalize his fear. Some prehistoric survival—an aquatic reptile that had dwelt for ages in this secret crater, untouched by the changes of evolution. It was possible, he knew. Always there had been tales of such monsters filtering through the jungles, gigantic beasts that dwelt in the Patagonian swamps and the hidden fastnesses of the Andes. Yet he could not control the cold horror that crept over him at sight of the thing that was emerging from the lake.

Its body was over fifty feet long, torpedo-shaped, with great flippers that propelled it slowly forward. The snake-like head and neck writhed, curved. All over its shining, reticulated body grew algae; shells clung to the armored hide. It came plunging up into the village, and the Curupuri went stampeding in a frenzied panic that made them easy prey for their god.

The two natives holding Mason went with the rest. Only Zol stood his ground, glaring around, bruised lips working silently. He saw Mason. He sprang forward, knife upraised.

This time Mason was ready. Grinning unpleasantly, he dived at the priest, tackling him viciously. Zol stabbed down with his knife, sending a white-hot streak of agony along Mason's ribs.

The white man clutched his enemy's wrist, held it motionless. Yelling rage, Zol bent his head, tried to sink his teeth in Mason's throat.

The screams of the fleeing Curupuri came up from below. And a cry—closer, nearer! Alasa!

"Kent! The devil-god—it's coming here—"

The sweating, bloody face of Zol was a gargoyle mask; the man's breath was foul in Mason's nostrils as the priest tried to reach his enemy's throat with his teeth. Beyond, a gargantuan shadow in the moonlight, Mason saw the head of the monster—coming closer!

Mason let go of the other's knife-wrist. Zol was not expecting that move. Before he could recover, the white man had gripped the priest by neck and crotch, hurled him up in midair. Mason's muscles cracked under the strain. He spun about swiftly, staggering.

The priest tried to stab down, missed. He had no other chance.

Out of the night came rushing the devil-god, silent and menacing. The huge head was not twelve feet from the pyramid's summit when Mason let go of his captive.

And sent Zol hurtling straight for the monster!

His aim was true. The jaws dipped slightly, and gripped the priest. One agonized shriek Zol gave, and then his bones and flesh were ground into pulp between remorseless fangs.

Mason waited to see no more. There was no time to free the girl; he leaped to the throne, picked up her bound, nude form, and slung it over his shoulder, hoping that Alasa would suffer no injury by such treatment. But it was that or death, for already the monster's head was snaking out as Mason leaped down the pyramid's side, keeping his balance with difficulty. He was trying to reach the passage that led into the structure, and he succeeded just as the giant reptile's jaws clicked closer than Mason cared to guess.

But they were safe, for the monster could not reach them in the narrow tunnel. Mason retreated further into the darkness, warily trying to pierce the gloom. Other Curupuri might have retreated here. Perhaps, though, their panic fear had driven all thought but instant flight from their minds.

Later Mason realized that this was indeed the case. But at present he was busy freeing Alasa, comforting her hysterical tears as well as he could. There was no sound from outside; either matters had quieted down, or it was difficult to hear within the pyramid. Mason drew Alasa close, and she, too frightened and exhausted to resist, relaxed in the man's arms, and, presently, slept. Mason did not arouse her. Though his

position was cramped, he endured it, fearing that any movement on his part would waken the girl.

When an hour or more had passed, he judged it time to
move.

"Alasa," he whispered. She stirred.

"Kent? What's wrong?"

"Nothing," he told her. "But we'd better be moving."

The girl arose and followed Mason to the portal. Peering
out into the moonlit night, they could see nothing of the
Curupuri, though a distant commotion in the jungle hinted of
the monster's activity. Mason was quick to act. Seizing
Alasa's hand, he hurried around the pyramid's base and
slipped through the village, keeping carefully in the shadows.
Once the girl paused to pick up a discarded length of cloth
and wrap it about her nude body. Both of them, shivering in
the cool night air, would have been glad to search for warmer
clothing, but they dared not spare the time.

They headed for the pass in the crater's walls. "You can
reach it in the fourth part of a day," the priestess had said. If
anything, she had overestimated the distance. Presently Alasa
and Mason reached the gap, having seen nothing of either the
Curupuri or the monster.

Below them lay a broad stretch of moonlit jungle, slanting
down to a distant horizon. Far, far beyond that horizon,
Mason guessed, lay the Atlantic Ocean, the Ocean Sea of a
pre-Columbian Europe. For a moment a queer thought was
strong in his mind; he would like to visit that lost, strange
world, dim in the forgotten past. How odd it would be to see
and speak with the legendary figures of history!

He saw the time-ship. Half a mile away, it lay in a little
clearing in the forest, the moon rays reflecting from it in a
blaze of cold brilliance. Mason wished he had brought a
weapon. There might be jaguars—perhaps even the
prehistoric giant sloth lumbered through this teeming jungle.

Night-prowlers were abroad, but they did not menace the two humans. Once some beast stalked them for a while; they could hear it rustling in the underbrush. But it gave up presently and disappeared. And once a jewel-bright macaw fluttered sleepily across their path, screaming its harsh cry.

But they came to the ship without hindrance. The Curupuri had apparently feared to enter it, for Mason found nothing amiss within the craft. He felt oddly relieved when he had closed the port, locking Alasa and himself within.

"I hope nothing was wrecked when we crashed," he told the girl. "It wouldn't be—pleasant."

Mason set to work examining the instruments. For more than an hour he puzzled over the intricate dials and gauges. Something he had learned from Greddar Klon, and more from Murdach. So, after a time, he felt that it might be possible to return to the future-world from which they had come.

"This dial," he said slowly, "indicates our time-rate, I think. Each time we stop, a permanent record of that halt is marked on the dial—those red spots, see? This one, at zero, is your own world, I imagine, where the ship was built. This dot, further up, is right under the needle. That's where we are now. And the third dot is where we left Murdach and Erech. If I can set the controls to that time-sector—"

It was another half-hour before Mason was satisfied. He tested the mechanism, lifted the ship fifty feet into the air. The atomic power worked smoothly enough. With a grim nod at Alasa, Mason threw the time switch.

Blackness. A second, an hour, or an eon—a brief eternity in which there was no consciousness of time. Then light came again.

The tower of the giant ants sprang into visibility nearby. They had reached their destination. The amazingly accurate controls of the craft had brought them back to the lost world of the future. But something was wrong.

From the tower's summit a horde of giant winged ants were pouring down, racing toward the ship. On the ground below lay the crushed form of another monster. But of Murdach and Erech there was no trace!

Instantly Mason guessed the reason. They had come too far—a few moments, or a few hours. No longer, certainly. His familiarity with the instruments helped him now. He made a quick adjustment and again moved the time-control.

Blackness—and light. The ship had apparently not moved. Only the Sun was in a different position in the sky, and the horde of ants had gone. Looking down, for a brief incredible moment Mason saw a replica of the time-ship, with two figures in it, rushing forward, colliding in mid-air with a huge ant. And as he watched—the ship vanished!

It was gone—back, Mason knew, to the pre-Columbian South American jungle. The ant, crushed, was falling toward the ground—toward two figures, missing them by a few feet. Erech and Murdach!

They waved tiny hands upwards, gesticulating. Mason sent the ship down, grounded it, flung open the port. Toward the craft raced the two men, eyes wide with hope they had long abandoned.

Erech pushed Murdach aboard, sprang after him. "By El-lil!" he swore. "You come in time, Ma-zhon! Let's get out of here, quick!"

Murdach was fumbling with the controls. The time-ship lifted, lanced across the desolate plain.

At last the four were reunited. Now—now, Mason thought triumphantly, they could seek Greddar Klon. Seek the Master—and slay him!

CHAPTER TWELVE
Strange Quest

The ship hung above the leaden sea, safe from attack, while the four talked, and Murdach and Mason planned. Murdach's tattered leather uniform was hanging in rags. His hawk-face was gaunt and tired; his red hair dark with grime. But Erech seemed unchanged. His pale eyes watched coldly above the beak of a nose; the thin lips were grim as ever.

"What I can't understand," Mason observed, "is how I got from Arabia—Al Bekr—to South America, a continent on the other side of the globe. I was moving in time, not in space."

"Globe?" murmured Alasa, puzzled. "Surely the Earth is flat, surrounded by an abyss?"

Murdach said, "You traveled in space, too. In a million years, or more or less, the world travels with the Sun, naturally, along its orbit. But the gravitational drag keeps the ship bound to Earth, which is lucky or we might find ourselves in space, light-years from any Solar System. The ship's bound—but not too tightly. The Earth revolves; the time-ship lags; and so you found yourself once in Al Bekr, once in—what did you say?—South America, and once here. But all three places are near the equator."

He turned to pages of calculations. "I've located Greddar Klon, I think. But nothing's certain. We cannot stay here, though, or we'll starve to death soon enough. Shall we—?" He read the answer in the other's eyes. Without speaking he sent the ship into time.

The light failed, and grew again. They hung above a craggy mountain range, gigantic, towering to the sky. The

Sun was warmer, closer and larger. Earth was green again, lacking the dead, leaden grimness of the ultimate future.

"This is before my own time, and after yours, Mason," Murdach said. "About 2150."

"2150 AD? That was Nirvor's time-sector," Mason said, remembering the words of the silver priestess. He went on, as a sudden thought came to him, "Hadn't we better find weapons first? In my time I can dig up a few—machine-guns, bombs—and you probably have better ones in your time, Murdach."

The other looked at him oddly, a curious expression in his eyes. "My time—I do not wish to return to it. Not yet, at least. As for weapons, the Master will not be expecting us. And we can perhaps find arms on our way. The needle points to the east, and we must go there. We'll watch as we travel."

Mason was not satisfied, but said no more. He scanned the barren mountains and plains, the teeming jungles, the lakes and broad sea over which they fled. Once he saw a gleaming globe on a mountaintop, and pointed it out to Murdach. The other brought the ship down.

A transparent globe, miles in diameter, hanging in empty air. Within it, as they hovered, Mason could see unfamiliar looking machines, rows upon rows of long cylinders of glass. Within the cylinders were human beings, men and women, dead or asleep.

Murdach landed the ship, and they tried to find some way of entering the giant globe, but in vain. There were no openings, and the transparent substance was steel-hard.

"We have a legend of this," Murdach said. "In the days of beast rule, ages ago, when experimenters sought to create human beings out of animals. Mankind foresaw some danger, a temporary warning of the solar rays, I think. They built huge spheres and sealed themselves within, throwing themselves into suspended animation for years. A few scientists tried to adapt themselves to the changing radiation, and spent their time making beasts into men, having some thought of creating an empire of their own to defeat the sleepers when they awakened. But they failed."

"We can't get weapons here," Mason grunted. "That's sure, anyway."

"There was some weapon those last scientists perfected," Murdach mused. "It was lost, forgotten. Only its power was remembered. No shield could bar it. If we could find that weapon and use it against Greddar Klon—" His eyes were alight.

"You need such magic to battle the Master," said Erech. "My scimitar would fail. I know that!"

The ship rose, drifted on. A jungle slipped beneath. Far away, steadily growing nearer, was a city—and Mason caught his breath at its heartbreaking beauty. Not Rome or Babylon nor Capri had ever had the delicate, poignant splendor of this strange metropolis, hidden in the jungle, crumbling and cracked with age at closer view, but still a matchless jewel of architecture.

"A rose-red city half as old as time," Mason quoted softly, half to himself.

The ship drove down. There was furtive movement in the jungle metropolis—not human movement. Animals scurried from sight. A leopard loped swiftly away. Birds flew startled.

"Greddar Klan is close," Murdach whispered. "My instruments show that."

The ship landed in a marble street. Hesitating, Mason opened the port, stepped out. Nothing happened. The still, humid air was utterly silent.

Far away a beast cried, lonely and strangely poignant. In the distance Mason saw a human figure. It came forward slowly, with a shambling, dragging gait. A man—an old man.

An Oriental, Mason guessed, noting the distinctive shape of the eyes, the facial contours, the hue of the skin. The oldster's face was withered, shrunken and dry as a walnut. Sparse white hair patched the skull. The thin lips moved endlessly, whispering. Filmed eyes dwelt unseeingly on Mason and the others.

But the man halted, and a new look came into his face. He spoke louder, in a language Mason thought he recognized. It was Chinese, but oddly changed, with a different stress and accent. Yet if Chinese had persisted for so many centuries, there was no reason why it should not exist in 2150 AD. Two hundred years would have made little difference.

The Chinese man said, "The Sleepers have awakened, then?"

Guessing at his meaning, Mason replied carefully, "We are not Sleepers. We come from another time—another age."

The man closed his eyes; tears trickled from the wrinkled lids. "I thought I had been forgiven. Ah, we have been punished indeed."

"Punished?"

"When the Sleepers went to their globes of refuge, we refused to join them. We thought to build a kingdom of beast-men. We reared cities for them, took possession of those already existing. We raised up the beasts...but that was long ago. Only a few are left now. They warred one upon another; slew and were slain...so now I, Li Keng, live alone in Corinoor, since Nirvor went across the desert with her leopards..."

Murdach had caught the familiar names. "Nirvor?" he broke in. "Ask him more of this, Mason! Is she here? What does he say?"

"I have met Nirvor," Mason said in Chinese. "She is alive, I think. You are her friend?"

Li Keng did not reply. Into his eyes crept a dull gaze. His lips twitched, writhed. He mumbled wordlessly. Suddenly he broke into a maniacal cackle of laughter.

A chill shook Mason. The oldster was mad!

Li Keng sobered. He ran skeletal fingers through his thin hair. "I am alone," he murmured. "Have the Sleepers forgiven? Did they send you?"

"We are from another time," Mason said, striving to pierce the mists about the dulled brain.

"The Sleepers? Have they—forgiven?" But Li Keng had lost interest. His low, insane laughter rang out again.

Apparently the man knew nothing of Nirvor or Greddar Klon, though Mason could rot be sure. He touched the Chinese's shoulder.

"Is there food here? We are hungry."

"Eh? There is fruit in the forest, and good water."

"Ask him of the weapon!" Murdach whispered. "Ask him!"

Mason obeyed. Li Keng peered through rheumy eyes.

"Ah, yes. The Invincible Power. But it is forbidden...forbidden."

He turned to go. Mason stepped forward, gripped the oldster's arm gently. The other tried feebly to disengage it.

"We mean no harm," Mason explained. "But we need your help. This Invincible Power—"

"You are from the Sleepers? They have forgiven?"

Mason hesitated. Then he said slowly, emphatically, "The Sleepers sent us to you. They have forgiven."

Would the ruse work? Would the crazed brain respond?

Li Keng stared, his lips working nervously. A thin hand plucked at his scant hair.

"This is true? They will let me enter a globe of refuge?"

"Yes. But you betrayed them before. They demand that you prove your faith."

The Chinese shook his head. "They—they—"

"You must give them the Invincible Weapon as proof that you will not betray them again."

Li Keng did not answer for a long moment. Then he nodded. "Yes. You shall have it. Come."

He lifted a hand as Mason beckoned to the others. "They may not come."

"Why not?" The other's voice was suspicious.

"There are only two suits of protective armor. The radium rays would kill you unless these are worn. We must go down into the radioactive caverns beneath Corinoor..." Li Keng paused, and a dull glaze crept over his eyes. Swiftly Mason translated.

"I don't dare cross him now. Might set him off his head entirely. You three stay with the ship—guard it till I get back with the weapon."

"But Kent..." Alasa's face was worried. "There may be danger—"

"Not from Li Keng, at least," Mason smiled. "I can look out for myself. Even if I was sure there was danger, I'd have to go. Until we get the weapon, we're unarmed."

"Let him go," Murdach said quietly. Erech said nothing, but his brown hand tightened on his scimitar-hilt.

"Let us start, Li Keng," Mason told the old Chinese, and followed the other along the deserted marble street. Presently Li Keng turned into a half-ruined building, passing between sagging gates of bronze, curiously carved. He halted in the portal.

"You must wait," he said. "Only worshippers of Selene and the condemned may enter here. I must tell the goddess my plans."

Before Mason could reply he slipped through an inner door and was gone. Whispering an oath, Mason took a stride forward—and halted. He peered through the narrow crack left by the half-closed panel.

He saw a huge, dim chamber, cryptic with gloom, and towering at the further end a monstrous female statue. Li Keng was moving across the floor, and as Mason watched he dropped to hands and knees, supplicating himself before the idol.

Well, there was nothing to fear from a goddess of stone or metal. Grinning crookedly, Mason drew back, and caught his breath as he heard a tumult from outside. An angry shout—

With a leap Mason reached the bronze doors. He peered out. His stomach moved sickeningly at the sight before him.

Dozens of malformed, half-human figures filled the marble street. They milled uncertainly about the time-ship, and in their midst were two round, prostrate figures—Alasa and Murdach. Coming toward Mason was—Greddar Klon!

The Master, moving forward with quick, hurried steps, pointed jaw set, eyes cold and deadly. Behind him came more of the strange creatures, being more bestial than human, Mason sensed. He then remembered the weird science that had changed animals to men, and guessed that the malformed, hairy, brute-faced monsters were products of that eerie experiment. Simultaneously Mason knew what he must do.

He saw Erech, scimitar red and lifted, running forward. The Sumerian roared a battle cry. He sprang at the Master, set himself for a stroke that, for all its force, could not penetrate the shielding atomic mesh.

Mason charged out through the bronze gates. He caught a glimpse of Greddar Klon whirling, involuntarily shrinking under the Sumerian's blow, lifting a metal tube in a tiny hand.

Mason's shoulder hit Erech, sent the giant driving aside. He flung himself on the Sumerian, striving to wrench the scimitar free, reading stark amazement in the other's pale eyes. Amazement—and anger, red rage that surged through Erech's veins and gave him strength enough to throw Mason down with ease. But the beast-men by now had surrounded the two.

Mason felt rough hands seize him. He made no resistance. Quietly he stood up, let the beast-men drag him toward Greddar Klon. Erech was still battling furiously, but without his scimitar he was handicapped. He went down at last, still struggling. His captors trussed him up with thongs.

The Master's cold eyes were probing. The shrill voice said, "Is Erech, then, your enemy, Mason?"

"Yes." The archeologist was playing for time. He had acted on impulse, knowing instinctively the best plan. But now he needed a chance to scrutinize his cards, to see which ones to play. He said, "Can we talk alone, Greddar Klon?" He nodded toward Erech.

For a long moment the other did not reply. Then he called a command, and two of the beast-men pulled Mason toward a nearby doorway. The Master followed.

Inside the building, in a fungus-grown, ill-smelling little room, Greddar Klon sat cross-legged on the floor. He signaled for the beast-men to release their captive.

"Thanks," Mason grunted. "There's a lot to explain. I didn't know if I'd ever find you."

"And now that you have—what?"

"Well—I still want to hold you to your bargain."

The other shrugged narrow shoulders. "Return you to your own time-sector?"

"Something more, now," Mason said quietly. "After you left Al Bekr, Erech asked me to help him release Alasa and Murdach. I did. Murdach explained your plans, that you intended to conquer a civilization and rule. My own civilization—isn't that so?"

"I, too, shall be frank," Greddar Klon conceded. "That is true."

"They wanted to find and kill you. Murdach built another time-ship. I helped him. I pretended to feel as they did. It wasn't difficult—for I wanted to find you, for reasons of my own. Back in Al Bekr I'd have been satisfied if you had returned me to my own time. But now, knowing what you intend, I want something more. I want a part in your kingdom, Greddar Klon!"

"I had thought of offering you that," the Master murmured. "But I did not need your aid."

"Are you sure? My world is unfamiliar to you. You will not know where to strike—what countries and cities to attack, what shipping and trade routes to block. I know my own world, and with my help, the information I can give you, you'll be able to subdue your enemies more swiftly and more easily."

"And you want?"

"Rule. Rule of a nation, under you, of course. I want power—"

The Master stood up. "I see. You are very clever, Kent Mason—but whether you are speaking the truth I do not know, as yet. You may be in earnest, and you may be trying to trick me. Until I have reached a decision, therefore, you will remain a prisoner—but safe."

He gestured. The beast-men seized Mason, pulled him out into the street. He made no resistance. He had planted a seed in Greddar Klon's mind, and now there was nothing to do but play a waiting game. He had not dared to bargain for the lives of Alasa and the others—that would have made the Master instantly suspicious.

His captors led him into another rose-marble building, and down to vaults far below. In a bare stone room he was locked. A torch set in the wall gave light, but how long it would last Mason did not know.

The shaggy, hulking forms of the beast-men lumbered out of sight. Mason was left alone, captive, his mind haunted with fear for his friends.

CHAPTER THIRTEEN
Court of the Beasts

After a time Mason rose and examined his prison. The walls, though cracked and lichened, were sturdy enough. The barred door was of metal, and too strong to force. Nor were ceiling or floor any more promising. Mason shivered in the chill air, wishing he had something warmer than a loincloth.

But the torch gave heat as well as light, until it expired. In the darkness it was somehow harder to judge time, though Mason guessed it was nightfall when at last one of the beast-men came with food. He poked it through the bars, a mess of fruits, specked and half-rotten, which Mason found it difficult to swallow. The beast-man brought a new torch, however.

It could not have been more than half an hour later that Mason saw a glimmer of light approaching. He went to the door, peering between the bars at a stooped, withered figure approaching. He made out a shriveled, Oriental face—Li Keng!

The Chinese man slowly unbarred the door. He beckoned Mason out.

"We must be silent," he mumbled in his cracked voice. "Nirvor has returned, and has brought an evil one with her. They seek the Invincible Power, but they do not know its hiding place. Nor do they know I hold the secret. Come!"

He shuffled along the corridor, his skinny hand gripping a torch. Mason kept pace with him.

"The others?" he asked softly. "My friends? Where are they?"

Li Keng did not hear. Hs wheezing voice went on, "Nirvor has brought the beast-men from the forest into Corinoor. But she shall not have the weapon. You shall take it to the Sleepers as proof of my faith."

Mason felt a pang of pity for the old man. They turned into another underground passage, and another, a veritable labyrinth, until Mason was hopelessly lost. Once he saw a white shadow slipping away in the distance, and remembered Valesta, Nirvor's leopard. But the beast did not reappear, if it had indeed been Valesta.

They stopped before a metal door. Li Keng fumbled in a recess in the wall, brought out two clumsy lead-sheathed suits. "We must wear these. The radium rays—"

Mason donned the garment. It had a transparent hood, which covered his head completely. The Chinaman, ungainly in the armor, pushed open the door.

They stood on the brink of a cliff that sloped down into a gray fog of distance. A narrow path ran perilously slanting down, and along this Li Keng started, keeping his balance without difficulty. Mason followed, with an inward tremor as he glanced aside into the dim gulf.

For perhaps a hundred yards they skirted the cliff, and then rounded a shoulder Mason paused, blinked blinded eyes. A flame of roaring brilliance blazed up from the gulf before him, and all through his body a curious tingling raced. The deadly radium radiations, he knew.

The path ran out on a spur of rock, narrow and dangerous, that hung over the abyss. Below it was a cauldron of fire, like the pit of a volcano. But more potent than liquid lava was the fire that burned here, having within the frightful power of radium!

A sound came from behind them. Mason turned. He cried out, his voice drowned in the roar of the inferno.

Stalking along the path toward him was Valesta, the white leopard.

Behind her—Nirvor, and at her heels the black leopard, Bokya. And dozens of the beast-men, fangs gleaming redly in the flame-light, eyes glowing.

From Li Keng came a cry so piercing that Mason heard it even above the thunder of the radium pit. The Chinese flung out an arm, gesturing Nirvor back.

The priestess laughed. Her silver hair floated unbound about her shoulders, half bared by her diaphanous black robe. She took a step forward.

Li Keng turned. He raced out on the spur. On its end he went on hands and knees, and then sprang erect, gripping a metal box in his gloved hands. Before the watchers could move Li Keng, gripping the box, had leaped out into the abyss!

A shriek came from Nirvor. Mason had a glimpse of her face, twisted into a despairing Gorgon mask—and then the white leopard was upon him. He went down under the onslaught. Only the width of the path here, at the base of the spur, saved him from toppling over. As it was, he hung for a moment on the brink, the leopard's weight bearing him down, the snarling beast-mask above his face.

Rough hands gripped him. The leopard leaped lightly away. Beast-men drew Mason back onto the ledge, lifted him to his feet. He was held motionless, facing the priestess.

She made a quick gesture, and Mason was forced back along the path. No use to resist, he knew. It would mean destruction, and even if he killed a few of his captors, he would inevitably be thrust into the gulf. So Mason let the beast-men pod him back to the metal door, where they stripped the armor from him.

Nirvor's face was white. "I have dared much," she whispered. "Men do not live long above the radium pit. A little more, and I would have died…horribly!" She shuddered, running white hands along her slender body.

The white leopard muzzled her leg, was thrust aside by the black one. The priestess said, "I thought Li Keng had the secret, and so I watched him. But he has destroyed the Invincible Power, and himself with it. He is beyond my reach. But you—you are not, Kent Mason!" A red blaze was in her jet eyes.

"We hold court tonight," she murmured. "Your three friends will die then. And you will die with them."

She gestured. The beast-man thrust Mason forward. Silently he let himself be taken back along the interminable corridors, back to his cell. But Nirvor did not pause there. Up and up they went, till at last they emerged in the streets of Corinoor.

"In here," the priestess commanded.

Mason recognized the building—the same one into which Li Keng had led him earlier that day. In the moonlight its ruin was not evident; it seemed a veritable palace of enchantment, a symphony in marble.

Through the bronze gates they went, through the inner door. The huge chamber was no longer dim. It was ablaze with torches, swarming with the beast-men. At the further end was a gigantic statue of a nude female form, moon-crowned.

Nirvor made a gesture toward the image. "It is Selene," she said. "Goddess of Corinoor—Corinoor that is soon to rise again in its former splendor!"

The priestess paused before a panel in the wall. It opened at her touch, and she pointed within.

"Go there, Kent Mason. Quickly!"

He obeyed, finding himself in a dusky, luxuriously furnished little room, ornate with tapestries and cushions. A small image of Selene stood in an alcove in the wall. The air was curiously dark, heavily scented with perfumes that rose headily to Mason's brain. He turned.

Nirvor stood alone before the closed door. Her black eyes dwelt on him cryptically.

"I have told you—you must die," she said.

"I heard you," Mason grunted. "So what?"

"I—have hated you. I have reason to do so. My kingdom, my goddess, my city of Corinoor—these I worship. For them I would destroy you utterly. Yet—" The jet eyes were strange, strange! "Yet you remember something I told you long ago in Al Bekr. I am woman…"

She made a hopeless gesture. "Now my heart is sick within me. For I know you should die, I know you hate me—"

The priestess dropped to the floor, her silver hair unbound veiling her face. *"Ohe, ohe!"* she sobbed. "In all my life I have known no man like you. There were the scientists, like Li Keng—and the barbarians of Al Bekr—and Greddar Klon. And the beast-man. I am woman, Kent Mason! I long for something I have never known…and that is love."

Mason did not reply. The honey-musk perfume was very strong. He felt oddly detached from his body, slightly drunk. He did not move when Nirvor arose and came toward him. She drew him down into the cushions.

Cool hands were against his cheeks; a flame-hot mouth avid on his own. And the strange eyes were close…

Once more Mason read a message in them—a—message of alienage! He drew back.

"You fear my eyes," Nirvor whispered. "But you do not fear my body…"

She stood up, her gaze hidden by long lashes. She fumbled at the fastenings of her black robe, let it fall in a lacy heap about her ankles. Mason caught his breath at sight of the priestess' voluptuous body. His throat was suddenly dry and parched.

Nirvor sank down again, her eyes closed. Her hands touched Mason's face, guided his lips to her own.

Something clicked in Mason's mind, like a blind springing up abruptly, letting light into a foul and darkened room. Immediately the dulling soporific spell of the perfumed incense was gone. For now Mason *knew*...

His stomach seemed to move sickeningly. He thrust the girl away. Her eyes glared into his.

Hoarsely Mason whispered, "I should have guessed the truth! What you and Li Keng and Murdach told me—"

Nirvor's lips were a scarlet wound in the pallor of her face. She shrilled, "You dare look at me like that! You dare—!"

"No. You don't like me to look at you now that I know. The scientists and their experiments—changing beasts into human beings—God!" Mason was shuddering as he remembered the passion the girl's body had aroused in him. He went on softly, unsteadily, "You are the outcome of such an experiment, Nirvor! You're not human. *You were a beast!*"

The priestess sprang up, bosom heaving, fingers clawed. "Aye! And what of that? They made me into a woman—"

Mason's face betrayed his horror. He whispered scarcely audibly, "What were you?"

Nirvor was silent for a moment. Then she said, "Bokya and Valesta—"

"The leopards?"

"They are my sisters!"

Her face contorted, Nirvor sprang to the door. She flung it open. From the great chamber beyond welled a deep-throated roar.

She cried a command. Beast-men poured into the room, seized Mason. Too sick with repugnance to speak, he fought desperately until weight of numbers bore him down, the foul odor of the beast-men strong in his nostrils.

Nirvor stood above him, a statue of living evil. Then she said, "You are proud of your humanity, Kent Mason? You may have cause to regret it. For now you come to the Court of the Beasts!"

The huge chamber was filled with surging multitudes of the beast-men. On a low dais before the statue of Selene, Mason saw, were three bound figures, Alasa, Murdach, and Erech. Mason was dragged to the dais, flung down upon it. Two beast-men held him motionless.

Nirvor stood beside him, a slim hand lifted. She cried something in the guttural language of the monsters. They roared a response.

"The verdict is death," the priestess said mockingly to Mason. "First—the girl. Prepare her, my people!"

She nodded, and a beast-man lifted the slim figure of Alasa, carried her into the midst of the horde. Shaggy, bestial figures closed around her. A scream broke from the girl.

Mason had a glimpse of rough hands loosening the cords, ripping the cloak roughly from Alasa. The girl was thrust upright, stood for a second staring wildly around, her bronze hair falling about her white shoulders. She cried out, held out imploring hands toward Mason. She took a few steps toward him—

The pack closed in, brutal hands mauling the girl's body. Cursing, Mason struggled with his captors. They held him motionless; their binding arms tightened, shutting off his breath. Gasping and sweating, Mason forced himself to relax.

Nirvor screamed a command. "The beast-men drew back slowly. One of them threw Alasa's body over his shoulder and loped toward the dais. The priestess pointed up.

A pulley hung from the roof, thongs dangling from it. The beast-man, in obedience to Nirvor's words, bound

Alasa's wrists tightly to the hanging ropes and then turned to a windlass near by. He turned it. Slowly Alasa was lifted till she swung by her hands, her hair falling like a veil over her face and breasts. Up and up, till her feet no longer touched the floor…

At last Nirvor nodded. The beast-man drew back. Alasa hung perhaps ten feet above their heads, a vision of tortured loveliness.

The priestess snarled at Mason, "*She* is human. But soon it will be difficult to be sure of that!"

Nirvor touched a lever. A grinding of machinery came from above. Staring up, Mason saw an arm of the image of Selene swing slowly down. God! Was Alasa to be crushed to death between the metal hands of the idol?

No, that could not be it, or both arms would be moving. The left arm of Selene halted about three feet from Alasa's dangling form. From the hand billowed a jet of white cloud—and the girl screamed in utter agony!

Steam! Live, boiling steam, hot enough to sear flesh from bone! Again Mason fought with his captors—and again they subdued him.

The hissing from above stopped. The steam had been on for only moments, but already Alasa's white body was flushed to a deep pink.

The image's arm swung back, lifted. The other arm descended slowly, with a ponderous creaking of gears. No steam issued from the metal palm, but Alasa's form writhed in pain, while a blast of chill air blew over Mason.

The torture of boiling steam, alternated with currents of icy, frigid air! This would be no quick death for Alasa, but a lingering hell of torment unendurable. She was sobbing softly, low moans of pain that made Mason feel sick and giddy.

"Nirvor!" he said urgently. "For God's sake, stop it! I'll do anything—"

"You are too late," the priestess whispered. In her jet eyes was torture-lust; on her face was stamped the cruelty of the beast. Her heritage, the leopard stigmata, was ruling now.

"Too late, Kent Mason! She shall die, and the others— but more quickly than you. Not for many moons shall you perish, and before you do you shall know the deepest pits of pain…"

Erech snarled a lurid oath, "Ma-zhon! Cannot you get free? These cursed ropes are too strong for me!"

Murdach's thin face was a pale, grimy mask of hopelessness. "They've destroyed the time-ship," he called. "Greddar Klon wrecked it."

Nirvor touched the lever again; once more the arm of the goddess began its slow descent. But before the live steam could jet forth there came an interruption. Into the chamber, through the open bronze doors, drifted a shimmering, transparent ovoid.

The time-ship of the Master! And within it—Greddar Klon!

CHAPTER FOURTEEN
Vengeance in Corinoor

The ovoid dropped beside the dais. Greddar Klon flung open the port, stood there, his cold eyes roving over the scene. He said harshly, "You take strange liberties, Nirvor."

As though sensing peril, black leopard and white slunk on to the dais, ranging themselves on either side of the priestess.

Nirvor said, "These captives are of no value."

"I am the judge of that! This man..." Greddar Klon pointed at Mason. "I told you to leave alone."

"I caught him With Li Keng, in the hiding place of the Invincible Power—"

"You found it?" Mason read eagerness in the Master's eyes. And so he spoke quickly, breaking in before Nirvor could answer.

"She lost it for you, Greddar Klon! She burst in on us with her leopards and beast-men, and Li Keng destroyed himself and the treasure rather than let it fall into Nirvor's hands."

"Is this true?" The Master glanced at the priestess.

"True—aye! As far as it goes. But ask him why he was seeking the Invincible Power. Ask him that!"

"I was seeking it for you," Mason said smoothly. "Li Keng set me free from my cell, told me he would not give the secret to you or Nirvor, I convinced him that I could guard the Power safely. I planned to secure it and give it to you, Greddar Klon, so you could know what my aid is worth."

"He lies!" the priestess spat. "He lies!"

"Set him free," Greddar Klon said. No one moved for a while. Then the Master's hand lifted, in it a metal tube. A beam of light flickered out, touched one of the beast-men that held Mason. The creature bellowed in agony, clawed at its chest—and dropped. It was dead.

The other beast-man waited for no more; he fled into the throng. The two leopards moved forward, guarding Nirvor with their bodies, green eyes baleful.

Mason swiftly turned to the windlass. He lowered Alasa to the dais, freed her wrists. Then he unbound Erech and Murdach.

Nirvor watched him, her lips a thin white line. Abruptly she turned on Greddar Klon, snarled, "I say this man lies! And I say he shall die—and the others."

The Master said in English, a language Mason did not realize he knew, "Come with me into the ship. Leave the others. Nirvor means to attack—and the beast-men will follow her."

Mason hesitated. His gaze went to the time-ship. Their own vessel had been destroyed, Murdach had said. Well—how could this situation be best turned to advantage?

Suddenly Mason knew. It would be a long chance, a desperate one, but the only one possible. With a sudden movement he sprang down from the dais and was at Greddar Klon's side.

His motion caused chaos. The priestess thrust out her arms, screamed a command. The leopards shot forward, snarling. The beast-men surged closer, and Greddar Klon hastily leaped into the ship. Mason followed him. The port slammed shut.

Through the transparent wall Mason could see Erech thrust Alasa behind him, guarding the girl with his body. Murdach was not in sight. Mason looked around.

He blessed the hours he had spent mastering the time-ship's controls. This vessel was identical in construction.

Greddar Klon was at the controls. He touched a button. The ship lifted, hung a dozen feet above the floor, out of reach of the beast-men.

Mason saw the lever he had been searching for. He sidled close to it. Briefly he felt an impulse to depend on his muscles to overcome Greddar Klon, but he knew that me Master's atomic mesh armor was impregnable. No, it must be this way—or failure.

There was a sudden tension in the air within me ship, a gentle breeze that brushed Mason's face. Greddar Klon turned. For the first time Mason saw emotion on that tiny, mask-like face. Bewilderment, apprehension, rage twisted the slitted mouth. The dwarf took a step forward.

And paused, gasping.

The air pressure was changing.

Mason had adjusted the atmospheric controls within the vessel, and now compressed air was pumping into the ship at dangerous speed. He had considered exhausting the air, creating a vacuum, but he knew that increased pressure would be far more harmful to Greddar Klon. And to himself, also! Already an intolerable weight was pressing in his eyes and ears; he found it almost impossible to breathe. The atmospheric pressure bore down on his chest, expelling air with a rush. It was incredibly difficult to draw another breath.

Greddar Klon's tiny mouth was wide as he gasped for air. He clutched at his belt, brought up the ray-tube. A searing yellow beam darted out at Mason. He twisted aside.

The ray swung toward him. Blood pumped painfully in his temples, and he felt blinding agony as the pressure began to collapse his capillaries and veins. The face of the Master seemed oddly distorted as Mason's eyeballs were crushed out of shape.

The ray seared his shoulder. Greddar Klon staggered forward. And then what Mason had been waiting for happened.

The huge cranium of Greddar Klon—burst!

Burst and spattered and hung in tatters like a smashed egg, the great brain, scarcely protected by a boneless membrane, crushed by the tremendous atmospheric pressure. The dwarfed body tottered and fell. With every movement agony, Mason managed to lift an arm, turn off the air pump. He reversed it, felt a breath of relief, was once more able to see.

Although Mason knew that sudden decrease of pressure could cause caisson disease, "the bends," he nevertheless sent the air pumping out as swiftly as he dared. Peering down through the transparent floor of the vessel, he saw the beast-men staring up, saw Nirvor near the dais, the leopards beside her. On the dais, unharmed, were Alasa, Murdach, and Erech.

Mason drove the ship down. Taking a chance, he swung open the door, and for a second felt sick and dizzy with the atmospheric change. But already beast-men were plunging toward him.

He whirled, scooped up the ray-tube from where it had fallen from Greddar Klon's fingers. Murdach and the others ran forward. Beast-men cut them off.

Mason burned them down with the heat-ray. A heavy weight landed on his back; he went down, the tube flying from his hand. Iron fingers dug into his neck.

Mason reached up and back, felt furry flesh under his hands. He bent forward suddenly, and the beast-man, taken by surprise, went hurtling down. His back hit the marble floor with a sickening crack. He lay still.

Mason looked around, Erech and Alasa were beside him, the girl's nude body still flushed with the steam-torture.

Murdach was running toward them, gripping the ray-tube Mason had lost.

The silver priestess stood on the edge of the dais, shrieking rage. Murdach turned and saw her.

He lifted the heat-ray. From the tube a yellow beam flashed out.

And Nirvor, the beast-woman, priestess of Selene in Corinoor, stood frozen for a brief second, and then dropped down silently and lay dead upon the marble.

The black leopard screamed, a cry that turned Mason a little sick, for he knew the relationship between Nirvor and the leopard. The beast charged straight for Murdach.

He killed it with the heat-ray.

Then he turned and came running toward the ship, scrambling with the others through the open port, slamming it shut, lifting the vessel into the air as a white fury raved and snarled against the transparent walls—the leopard Valesta. The beast-men surged in, in a mad charge that was insane with rage. Half-involuntarily Mason touched the controls, sent the ship into time. The fantastic scene outside was hidden by a curtain of darkness.

The black veil lifted. They hung once more in the temple of Selene—but it was empty now. The bronze gates were ajar, and through them a pale, chill radiance crept wanly. Nor were there torches burning in the temple.

It was dark—and cold, cold!

Age had dropped down upon it.

"We are in the future," Murdach whispered, with a glance at the dials. "A jump of ten years—"

That hell of battle that had raged a moment ago was, in reality, ten years in the past, Mason knew. Silently he brought the ship down. At his feet was the mangled body of Greddar Klon, and he put this outside the ship, without looking at the ruined head and face.

"We cannot stay here long," Murdach said. "The solar radiation has waned. I think life will not exist long on the Earth, save in the globes of refuge. It will be a hundred years and more before the Sun regains its former brightness and the Sleepers awaken. But let us see what ten years has done to Corinoor."

"Is it safe?" Alasa whispered.

"Safe enough," Murdach told her. He led the way out of the ship.

Gloom shadowed the great temple. The jungle had encroached with weeds and fungi and grasses; one of the arms of the statue of Selene had fallen. It was utterly silent.

Alasa came into the circle of Mason's arm. She was shivering.

Murdach said, "One moment. I have something to tell you."

Mason turned. Murdach was standing beside the port of the ship, a dozen feet away. He held the heat-ray in his hand.

His red hair looked black in the shadow. "Don't come any nearer," he went on. "I do not wish to kill you. I prefer to leave you here, alive."

Unbelievingly Mason took a step forward. Murdach's hand steadied. The ray-lube was aimed at his middle.

"Stop where you are!" the other said warningly. "I mean it!"

"Murdach!" Alasa gasped. "What are you doing?"

"Doing? I'm doing what Greddar Klon planned. You never knew why I didn't wish to return to my own time. I'm an outlaw there, a hunted criminal. I tried to overthrow the rulers, and escaped only by flight across the desert, where the time trap caught me. Oh, you've aided me, the three of you—aided me in overcoming Greddar Klon. But now that he's dead, it will be possible for me to do as he intended—conquer a time-sector and rule it!"

"You dog!" Erech roared, pale eyes blazing. "You foul traitor!"

"Say what you like—but come no nearer, or you'll die. The Master's plan shall be carried through as he intended, with this difference—I'll take his place. As for you three, I shall be merciful. I'll leave you here. Perhaps you will live for a time. Perhaps the decreased solar radiation will kill you soon."

Mason felt Alasa's slim, nude body shrink against his. His throat felt dry and tight. To fail now, through Murdach's betrayal, after their struggle! The idea was insupportable.

Mason glanced at Erech, caught a look of understanding in the Sumerian's eye. They would attack at the same time. Murdach would certainly kill one of them, but perhaps the other...

Murdach realized their intention. His jaw tightened. He lifted the ray-tube as Mason's muscles tensed.

And then—out from the shadows charged the impossible! A white, roaring thunderbolt that crashed down on Murdach and sent the man toppling back, struggling vainly against the creature. Instantly Mason knew.

Valesta, the white leopard! For ten years she had lurked in the temple, watching and waiting for the man who had slain the silver priestess. And now, after a decade, he had returned to the fangs and claws of vengeance.

The heat ray blazed out. Flesh ribboned under tearing talons. From Murdach came a shrill, agonized cry that screamed up and up unendurably, and ended suddenly in a choking, wordless sound that was sheer horror.

Then it was over. Man and leopard lay still and silent. Unmoving—dead!

Mason felt a queer sense of unreality as he closed the port of the time-ship after he followed the others aboard. He glanced out at the vast, gloomy temple of Selene, sagging into dark ruin. There was an overwhelming awe upon him as he thought of the countless lives that had existed in dead Corinoor, the incredible multitude of people that would dwell upon Earth until the last man gasped out his breath in the chill twilight of a heatless, lightless planet.

He shuddered involuntarily. Alasa moved close, her golden eyes tender. Mason, glancing down, felt his depression leave him.

"Alasa," he said softly, "what now?"

"We can return—" The girl's voice was hesitant.

"Return—bah!" Erech grunted. "I am tired of Al Bekr, Ma-zhon. Also I am tired of my world. This world of yours, now—I should like to see it. And I should like to be with you. But—" He hesitated, an odd look in the pale eyes. "But I serve you, Alasa. If you wish me to go back to Al Bekr— why, I shall keep faith. But, by El-lil, Ma-zhon is a man to cleave to!"

"I think you are right," the girl said. "But what does Mason think of this?"

For answer Mason took a step forward, gripped the Sumerian's brown hands. "We have fought well together," he said, "and we would have died together. All that I have is yours, Erech. If you come with me, I do not think you'll regret it."

"And I?" Alasa broke in. Mason turned.

"You will go back to Al Bekr, I suppose," he said, a dull ache in his throat at the thought of losing the girl. "I know how to work the time-ship. I can—"

"Oh, Kent—you fool!" Alasa murmured. "We too have fought together and would have died together. My people are safe in Al Bekr now. Nothing draws me back there. But— would you let me join you and Erech?"

For answer Mason took Alasa into his arms. "Let you? It's the only thing I want. But I didn't dare ask—"

131

The girl gave a little chuckle as she leaned her bronze curls against Mason's shoulder. "I would not have let you escape me, Kent. Never fear that!"

The Sumerian gave a deep-throated laugh. "Come, Ma-zhon! Let us start. I am anxious to see this world of yours."

"Okay," Mason smiled. "And if you don't like it—well, we still have the time-ship. Perhaps…"

He didn't finish. He touched the instrument panel, and the veil of blackness dropped down.

And Alasa kissed him.

THE END

If you've enjoyed this book, you will not want to miss these terrific titles…

ARMCHAIR SCI-FI & HORROR DOUBLE NOVELS, $12.95 each

D-91 **THE TIME TRAP** by Henry Kuttner
THE LUNAR LICHEN by Hal Clement

D-92 **SARGASSO OF LOST STARSHIPS** by Poul Anderson
THE ICE QUEEN by Don Wilcox

D-93 **THE PRINCE OF SPACE** by Jack Williamson
POWER by Harl Vincent

D-94 **PLANET OF NO RETURN** by Howard Browne
THE ANNIHILATOR COMES by Ed Earl Repp

D-95 **THE SINISTER INVASION** by Edmond Hamilton
OPERATION TERROR by Murray Leinster

D-96 **TRANSIENT** by Ward Moore
THE WORLD-MOVER by George O. Smith

D-97 **FORTY DAYS HAS SEPTEMBER** by Milton Lesser
THE DEVIL'S PLANET by David Wright O'Brien

D-98 **THE CYBERENE** by Rog Phillips
BADGE OF INFAMY by Lester del Rey

D-99 **THE JUSTICE OF MARTIN BRAND** by Raymond A. Palmer
BRING BACK MY BRAIN by Dwight V. Swain

D-100 **WIDE-OPEN PLANET** by L. Sprague de Camp
AND THEN THE TOWN TOOK OFF by Richard Wilson

ARMCHAIR SCIENCE FICTION CLASSICS, $12.95 each

C-31 **THE GOLDEN GUARDSMEN**
by S. J. Byrne

C-32 **ONE AGAINST THE MOON**
by Donald A. Wollheim

C-33 **HIDDEN CITY**
by Chester S. Geier

ARMCHAIR SCIENCE FICTION & HORROR GEMS SERIES, $12.95 each

G-9 **SCIENCE FICTION GEMS, Vol. Five**
Clifford D. Simak and others

G-10 **HORROR GEMS, Vol. Five**
E. Hoffman Price and others

If you've enjoyed this book, you will not want to miss these terrific titles…

If you've enjoyed this book, you will not want to miss these terrific titles…

ARMCHAIR SCI-FI & HORROR DOUBLE NOVELS, $12.95 each

D-21　**EMPIRE OF EVIL** by Robert Arnette
　　　THE SIGN OF THE TIGER by Alan E. Nourse & J. A. Meyer

D-22　**OPERATION SQUARE PEG** by Frank Belknap Long
　　　ENCHANTRESS OF VENUS by Leigh Brackett

D-23　**THE LIFE WATCH** by Lester del Rey
　　　CREATURES OF THE ABYSS by Murray Leinster

D-24　**LEGION OF LAZARUS** by Edmond Hamilton
　　　STAR HUNTER by Andre Norton

D-25　**EMPIRE OF WOMEN** by John Fletcher
　　　ONE OF OUR CITIES IS MISSING by Irving Cox

D-26　**THE WRONG SIDE OF PARADISE** by Raymond F. Jones
　　　THE INVOLUNTARY IMMORTALS by Rog Phillips

D-27　**EARTH QUARTER** by Damon Knight
　　　ENVOY TO NEW WORLDS by Keith Laumer

D-28　**SLAVES TO THE METAL HORDE** by Milton Lesser
　　　HUNTERS OUT OF TIME by Joseph E. Kelleam

D-29　**RX JUPITER SAVE US** by Ward Moore
　　　BEWARE THE USURPERS by Geoff St. Reynard

D-30　**SECRET OF THE SERPENT** by Don Wilcox
　　　CRUSADE ACROSS THE VOID by Dwight V. Swain

ARMCHAIR SCIENCE FICTION CLASSICS, $12.95 each

C-7　**THE SHAVER MYSTERY, Book One**
　　　by Richard S. Shaver

C-8　**THE SHAVER MYSTERY, Book Two**
　　　by Richard S. Shaver

C-9　**MURDER IN SPACE**
　　　by David V. Reed

ARMCHAIR MASTERS OF SCIENCE FICTION SERIES, $16.95 each

M-3　**MASTERS OF SCIENCE FICTION, Vol. Three**
　　　Robert Sheckley, "The Perfect Woman" and other tales

M-4　**MASTERS OF SCIENCE FICTION, Vol. Four**
　　　Mack Reynolds, Part One, "Stowaway" and other tales

If you've enjoyed this book, you will not want to miss these terrific titles...

If you've enjoyed this book, you will not want to miss these terrific titles…

ARMCHAIR SCI-FI & HORROR DOUBLE NOVELS, $12.95 each

D-61   **THE MAN WHO STOPPED AT NOTHING** by Paul W. Fairman
TEN FROM INFINITY by Ivar Jorgensen

D-62   **WORLDS WITHIN** by Rog Phillips
THE SLAVE by C.M. Kornbluth

D-63   **SECRET OF THE BLACK PLANET** by Milton Lesser
THE OUTCASTS OF SOLAR III by Emmett McDowell

D-64   **WEB OF THE WORLDS** by Harry Harrison and Katherine MacLean
RULE GOLDEN by Damon Knight

D-65   **TEN TO THE STARS** by Raymond Z. Gallun
THE CONQUERORS by David H. Keller, M. D.

D-66   **THE HORDE FROM INFINITY** by Dwight V. Swain
THE DAY THE EARTH FROZE by Gerald Hatch

D-67   **THE WAR OF THE WORLDS** by H. G. Wells
THE TIME MACHINE by H. G. Wells

D-68   **STARCOMBERS** by Edmond Hamilton
THE YEAR WHEN STARDUST FELL by Raymond F. Jones

D-69   **HOCUS-POCUS UNIVERSE** by Jack Williamson
QUEEN OF THE PANTHER WORLD by Berkeley Livingston

D-70   **BATTERING RAMS OF SPACE** by Don Wilcox
DOOMSDAY WING by George H. Smith

ARMCHAIR SCIENCE FICTION & FANTASY CLASSICS, $12.95 each

C-19   **EMPIRE OF JEGGA**
by David V. Reed

C-20   **THE TOMORROW PEOPLE**
by Judith Merril

C-21   **THE MAN FROM YESTERDAY**
by Howard Browne as by Lee Francis

C-22   **THE TIME TRADERS**
by Andre Norton

C-23   **ISLANDS OF SPACE**
by John W. Campbell

C-24   **THE GALAXY PRIMES**
by E. E. "Doc" Smith

If you've enjoyed this book, you will not want to miss these terrific titles...

ARMCHAIR SCI-FI & HORROR DOUBLE NOVELS, $12.95 each

D-71   **THE DEEP END** by Gregory Luce
         TO WATCH BY NIGHT by Robert Moore Williams

D-72   **SWORDSMAN OF LOST TERRA** by Poul Anderson
         PLANET OF GHOSTS by David V. Reed

D-73   **MOON OF BATTLE** by J. J. Allerton
         THE MUTANT WEAPON by Murray Leinster

D-74   **OLD SPACEMEN NEVER DIE!** John Jakes
         RETURN TO EARTH by Bryan Berry

D-75   **THE THING FROM UNDERNEATH** by Milton Lesser
         OPERATION INTERSTELLAR by George O. Smith

D-76   **THE BURNING WORLD** by Algis Budrys
         FOREVER IS TOO LONG by Chester S. Geier

D-77   **THE COSMIC JUNKMAN** by Rog Phillips
         THE ULTIMATE WEAPON by John W. Campbell

D-78   **THE TIES OF EARTH** by James H. Schmitz
         CUE FOR QUIET by Thomas L. Sherred

D-79   **SECRET OF THE MARTIANS** by Paul W. Fairman
         THE VARIABLE MAN by Philip K. Dick

D-80   **THE GREEN GIRL** by Jack Williamson
         THE ROBOT PERIL by Don Wilcox

ARMCHAIR SCIENCE FICTION CLASSICS, $12.95 each

C-25   **THE STAR KINGS**
         by Edmond Hamilton

C-26   **NOT IN SOLITUDE**
         by Kenneth Gantz

C-32   **PROMETHEUS II**
         by S. J. Byrne

ARMCHAIR SCI-FI & HORROR GEMS SERIES, $12.95 each

G-7   **SCIENCE FICTION GEMS, Vol. Four**
         Jack Sharkey and others

G-8   **HORROR GEMS, Vol. Four**
         Seabury Quinn and others

A NEW SPECIES OF PLANT LIFE ON THE MOON?

If a self-absorbed geologist was telling the truth, he had indeed made a radical discovery on the Lunar surface. But Dr. Jack Imbriano had his doubts. Just exactly where on the moon did geologist Milt Ingersoll find this new species of lichen? And with the destruction of the suspect plant samples, the whole Lunar crew began to wonder…was Ingersoll trying to perpetrate a hoax? If so, what was his motive and, more importantly, what would be his next move?

Ten men were sent to the Moon on an expedition to record the various Lunar resources. And in the end, ten men would fight valiantly to return safely back to Earth! Danger and intrigue abound in Hal Clement's cunning tale of one man's search for fame and another man's search for the truth.

CAST OF CHARACTERS

DR. JACK IMBRIANO
This physician thought there was something fishy about the new Lunar plant life. Was he right, or perhaps a little paranoid?

RAY KINCHEN
Astronomer, ballistic engineer, and leader of the crew—like it or not, he expected things to be done logically and with purpose.

MILT INGERSOLL
He claimed discovery of a new species of lichen on the moon. As a yet unknown geologist, were credentials his main concern?

AL DETZEL
By day just a regular joe pulling tractor duty, but by night he was irreplaceable as the crew's only fuel system expert.

BILL FRAKE
He knew there was real trouble ahead when he went to take his turn at galley duty…and found no food!

TICK WESLEY
Being the surliest, crankiest member of the crew, he wasn't exactly someone you wanted to hang out with after work.

THE LUNAR LICHEN

By
HAL CLEMENT

ARMCHAIR FICTION
PO Box 4369, Medford, Oregon 97504

*For more information about Armchair Books and products, visit our
website at...*

www.armchairfiction.com

Or email us at...

armchairfiction@yahoo.com

CHAPTER ONE

KINCHEN looked out and down from the observation port, watching the suited figure absorbed in its task about the trailer. He watched until the big number stenciled on the suit became visible, and he could be sure of the worker's identity; then he turned abruptly to the men seated behind him. His eyes sought out one of these. "You admit they were—and are—alive." It was more a statement than a question. Imbriano took it so.

"They are."

"And you don't recognize the species."

"I don't—but that's..." Kinchen raised a hand impatiently.

"I understand that you don't know by sight every fungus, lichen, or what have you that's ever been described. You can, though, recognize classes. And you think you recognize this one as belonging to whatever-you-call-it..."

"Hysteriales. And that's not..."

"Never mind. I didn't mean to get technical about orders and phyla and whatever you call them. I'm no biologist. The point is—or I think it is—that you used fairly gross characteristics for identification, and such characteristics might very well be duplicated by parallel evolution. Right?"

"That's true."

Ingersoll had gone out alone in the tractor, and the question was: what was he up to?

"Very well, then. Will you tell me why, except for a natural reluctance to believe there's any life at all, anywhere on the moon, you feel so strongly that Ingersoll is pulling a Piltdown on us? Don't you like the fellow, or what?"

JACK IMBRIANO hesitated, and frowned.

"It's true that I don't like him very much," he admitted finally, "but I don't *think* that's what had given me the idea. It's the whole set-up. He came back from a trip, which he'd made alone, well past our normal exploring range, with these specimens of lichen—or pseudo-lichen if you prefer. He had taken pictures of the site, but he says he took them *after* collecting the specimens, and the pictures certainly don't show any of the plants. They hardly could, of course, since the plants themselves are so small. He objects to going back to the site to find more..."

"He didn't object. I did," Kinchen pointed out. "We have just so much working juice for ground travel, and Ingersoll used too much of it as it is. We could draw a little from the main tanks, but I don't want to cut our return allowance too fine."

"All right, you objected. But he also said there was no use going back, because he'd collected all he could find in the vicinity. That's ridiculous, on several counts. First of all, they're so small he couldn't be sure he'd found all that were there, any more than you could pick all the raspberries from a patch the first time through. Secondly, he shouldn't have done it. Even a geologist leaves some of his material *in site* so that his work can be checked, as a standard working procedure. Under the circumstances, I want to go back to that region and hunt for more of what he found—if he found it."

THE DIRECTOR thought things over for a minute or so.

"Your point is well taken, but the fuel question remains," he said at last. "We can do it, of course, though it more than likely means canceling some other part of the program. Aren't there any more checks you could make right here, first? How about the rock the stuff is attached to? Correct me if I'm wrong, but don't lichens normally have some effect on the stuff they grow on—stick roots into it, and so on? How about checking that with the microscope."

"Lichens don't have true roots…"

"Stop quibbling. They keep from being blown and shaken off rocks and trees somehow."

"You're right—but these were growing on the dust layer, according to Ingersoll. He brought some of the dust with him, but it's not possible to say whether or not it's the original substrate of the plants."

"Well, if, as you imply, he brought them from Earth with him, there should be traces of Terrestrial soil mixed in with the things. Can't you identify that?"

"I can't. We have geologists here, but who thought we'd need a soil specialist?"

"True enough. All right—how about this? Put some of the plants outside, and see whether they live, and grow. You say they're alive now."

"They seem to be—as nearly as one can tell with a lichen. There is protoplasm or something like it, in their cells. And it shows streaming at times."

"Then do what I suggest. Ask Ingersoll whether he found them in full sunlight or in shadow—so he can't say you didn't reproduce conditions properly—put them out for a few hours, and see what happens."

"A few hours wouldn't produce detectable change in one of our lichens. Most of them take years to do much growing, as I remember."

KINCHEN chuckled. "I'm just an astronomer and ballistics engineer," he said, "but I'll bet that a few hours of this environment will do something detectable to any Terrestrial life form. If that thing is still alive, after a few hours outside, then it's genuine—whether it shows any growth or not. I know people have talked for years about lichen-like growths being possible here, but I never heard a competent man say that actual Terrestrial lichens themselves could stand it. They'd be cooked, irradiated to death, and desiccated in a matter of minutes, and you'll have a hard time convincing me otherwise. That's why I doubt that Milt could possibly be trying a fake. He'd know there are too many easy ways to check on him."

"Why would he know it? He's just a geologist."

"Why would *I* know it? I'm just an astronomer. I don't see how anyone sharp enough to make a name for himself in any one science can be completely ignorant of the rest."

"But Ingersoll hasn't made much of a name, even in his own profession."

"Then how come he's with us here?"

"How come I'm here? I passed a Civil Service exam."

"Hmph." Kinchen might have been impressed; it was hard to tell. "Get on with your check, anyway. If those things stay alive outside, I'll authorize another trip to the place he found 'em—where was it? Other side of Short, somewhere, didn't he say?"

"Right." Imbriano was already on his way down the hatch from the "main" deck.

At an observation port beside the main airlock there was a microphone, which was tied to the suit-frequency transmitter. The doctor snapped it on. "Milt? You read me?"

"Clear enough. What is it?" Ingersoll's voice came back instantly.

"I was wondering whether you'd found these plants in sunlight or shadow. It's a rather small sample, and it occurred to us that if we put some of them back outside—planted 'em, you might say—we could grow more before we have to leave, and learn more about them at the same time."

"I SEE." THERE was a pause, and Imbriano wondered whether the other was pursing his lips in his usual pontifical manner when asked a question, or trying to decide what answer would suit the situation best. "They were in sunlight when I found them," he said after a moment, "but I can't remember whether they were in spots which had been out of shadow for long, or not. None of them was very far from some sort of shadow—but of course nothing is, in this part of the moon. It's as rough on a small scale as it is on the large one of astronomical photographs."

"That's true." The doctor was suspicious of the answer—it sounded like hedging to him. Of course, almost any other answer would have been equally suspicious, and Imbriano might have been broad-minded enough to admit this if someone had taxed him with the idea.

"Certainly they'd been in the sun for hours, anyway, and maybe days," the voice from the radio resumed. "I guess your stunt is worth trying. From what little I know of lichens, though, they won't do much in the few hours the ship will be in the sun. Remember, we came down just about south of the central peak of this crater, and we'll be in its shadow before long."

"That's true. Well, the few hours will do for an initial test—maybe I'll be able to find out how the plants keep from drying out in this pressure and temperature, anyway. I'll be out shortly."

Imbriano broke the connection without waiting for an answer, and went back to the main deck. The specimens were on the small table, which served him for a laboratory. He had distributed them, together with the lunar dust, which had been brought in with them, over several plastic Petri dishes. He glanced over these, picked up two, which seemed to have healthy cultures in them, and carried them back down to the air lock deck. There he suited up, tested his gear, picked up the dishes again, and went through the air lock.

Getting down the ladder with his burden took some skill, the gripping attachments of the suits being what they were, but he managed it at last. Ingersoll's suited form was fifty yards away, still working over one of the tractor-trailer combinations; he did not seem too interested in the doctor's work. They exchanged a brief word over the suit radios, but the geologist did not leave his job.

IMBRIANO looked around for a suitable place to expose the specimens. The neighborhood of the ship was littered with gear, which had accumulated during the five days of their stay so far. Some of it was apparatus that would have to be returned to Earth; some, like auxiliary fuel tanks, was doomed to stay on the moon. He thought of setting the dishes in sunlight on top of one of the tanks, where it could easily be found again; then he remembered that the radiation equilibrium temperature of the polished metal was a good deal higher than that of the lunar rock, and he would hardly be duplicating natural conditions.

He finally selected a spot about thirty yards north of the ship, a small open area floored with the omnipresent lunar dust, set the dishes down, and removed their covers. He watched them for a minute or two; they showed no visible change, and he finally turned back toward the ship. He was startled to find Ingersoll just behind him, though he certainly shouldn't have expected to hear him coming.

"Hello, Milt," he greeted the geologist. "Does that seem an adequate replica of their growing conditions? You said they were on dust when you found them."

"That's right. I don't suppose the dishes will make any difference. Why did you have covers on them, before?"

"The general idea is to keep foreign spores from settling in a culture. I was reasonably careful about that, and of course there won't be too many drifting around in the ship anyway—they'd have been cycled through the purifying plant too many times by now. I suppose that spores from the algae in the plant itself might be loose, but I don't think the danger's very great. Anyway, if your specimens *have* been contaminated, they're getting well sterilized now."

"How's that?"

IMBRIANO gestured around them. "This environment. Temperature and pressure would combine to dry out any Earthly life form in minutes. Creatures which formed spores might have time to do so, but the spores would die of ultraviolet irradiation quickly enough—no Terrestrial life has natural immunity, as far as I know. Those of us who can take it do so by virtue of a relatively opaque protecting layer of dead tissue. That's one thing that interests me enormously about your plants—they must obviously have some other protection, or else a genuine immunity to ultra-violet light. That's why I want to grow more of them. There aren't enough now to spare for experiment. They're amazing enough things as it is."

"How come?" Neither Ingersoll's voice, nor the face, which could be seen inside the helmet, seemed unduly perturbed by the information that the doctor was deliberately providing.

"How come? Because even though they're adapted to the moon, they survived the pressure and oxygen concentration inside the ship. They were definitely alive when I examined them in there microscopically."

"Hmm. That is funny, now that you mention it. How do you account for it?"

"I don't yet. With more information, I suppose ideas will suggest themselves. I'll bring one of these dishes in just before the shadow of that peak reaches us, half a day or so from now, and leave the other one out to cool down in the dark. I'll settle on when to bring it in after I've examined the first one. That seems like a sensible program?"

"I'd say so. Let me know what you find out, will you? I'm a bit curious—after all, I found the things."

"Don't worry. It will be remembered to your credit." The doctor wondered whether he had worded that answer badly, but Ingersoll gave no evidence of thinking the remark at all odd. He turned with Imbriano and started back toward the ship.

"Finished your work?" the doctor asked.

"Not yet. Can't stay in a suit forever, though. It'll be nice to get back to a place where they can spare air for smoking."

Imbriano chuckled. "It isn't that we can't spare it, but that the algae in the 'fresher are too sensitive to tobacco smoke. If you really want fame, breed a variety with comparable photosynthetic efficiency, which can stand a few impurities of that sort. The submarine boys will probably give you an honorary commission." The conversation broke off here, as climbing the ladder to the air lock took too much of a man's attention for other matters to intrude.

THE TWO reached the main deck together, so there was no opportunity for those already there to ask the questions they would have liked; but the doctor made the general situation clear easily enough.

"We put the dishes out in the sun, and I'll bring in the first one just before the shadow gets here. Until then, I guess there's nothing to be done."

"Listen to him," groaned one of the men. "Nothing to be done! Whoever planned this junket accounted for every minute of every man's time—except, of course, that of the good old M. D. I see him sitting around a good deal."

"You don't look too occupied yourself Tick," retorted Imbriano. "That chair you're in seems pretty comfortable." This remark left him wide open, since all the "chairs" were bucket seats fastened firmly to the frame of the rocket. The crewman ignored the opportunity, however.

"I'm sitting," he said, "because it's a lot easier than standing while my suit tanks are getting charged. I brought in a trailer load of specimens about half an hour ago. Al and someone else immediately refueled the tractor and took it out again, this time with a different trailer. As soon as my suit is ready—and I've had a chance to digest the sandwich I just ate—I'll get into my suit again and, with such help as I can get from anyone whose time isn't planned, I'll unload and catalogue the said specimens. If I should finish that before it's time to sleep…"

"All right, you've made your point. I'll help with your cataloguing, if it doesn't take any more knowledge of mineralogy than I possess, and if no one develops a cold I have to treat in the meantime."

"WHO'S BEEN sick so far? It's disgusting, how some people get paid for their vacations. I'll use your help. It doesn't take any brains."

The conversation wandered from that point, and both talk and labor bore little relation to the Ingersoll discovery for some hours afterward. Most of the time, the people were outside; all the work, or practically all of it, lay there. Even the physical measurements, which did not actually demand samples of the moon, were usually better made away from the metal of the hull. One man always remained aboard, as a safety measure, but this duty was taken in turn.

Tractors and trailers came and went; the trailer system permitted almost continuous use of the powered vehicles. The trailers were light affairs, having three pairs of very low-pressure balloon tires, with interchangeable bodies. They could be used for hauling equipment or specimens of virtually any sort; and of course at least one always carried "fuel"—working fluid for their nuclear turbines.

Theoretically, one tank of the fluid should last indefinitely, since the turbine exhaust was condensed and recycled; practically, there were always losses—the fluid was ordinary water, which was decomposed quite rapidly in the reactor. Also, occasional use of "emergency power" demanded a cycling rate greater than the condensers could always handle, since they could only get rid of heat by radiation. At such times automatic valves opened the condensers briefly to "outside" and fluid would be lost. One trailer tank could usually be counted on for around three or four hundred miles of ordinary travel, but no one took the figure too much for granted.

There were pairs of investigators radiating in all directions about the crater. The central peak was receiving particular attention; it was one of the highest on the moon, a peculiarity of Moretus, and central peaks in general were still being used as ammunition in the perpetual fight between the meteoriticists and the endogenecists over the question of Lunar crater origin. A topographic map of the crater, with five-foot contour intervals and complete geological information on what underlay the contours, was the group's aim: while the mapping itself would not be done on the site, a fantastic amount of measuring had to be. The photographic technicians had hardly been seen since the landing; they had been eating and sleeping in their laboratory, which had been set up in one of the used fuel tanks away from the ship.

As a result, not even Jack Imbriano gave a thought to the lichen specimens, or even to his ugly, growing suspicion about Ingersoll, for a good many hours. When he did, the recollection was forced on him; the shadow of the mile-and-a-half-high central peak was nearing the pillar of the rocket, and most of the teams were coming in—the first time since the start of the project that so many had been in together. Recalling his plan for the plant specimens, the doctor suited up and went after them himself—he was not going to let anyone else touch them.

Unfortunately, he was a trifle late. It was a little hard to identify the remains of the Petri dishes and plants in the layer of dust where they had been left, and which had subsequently been traversed by the treads of one of the tractors.

CHAPTER TWO

IMBRIANO stood and thought. True, he had not put up a flag, or issued any other general warning to the crews about his little experiment; that he had to admit. On the other hand, the spot was unusually close to the ship, and the changing of trailers was usually accomplished in one area a little distance away. It was not impossible—for an objective mind, it would not even have been unlikely—for a tractor to cross the spot, but Imbriano was suspicious. He raked through the dust once more, seeing a few fragments of plastic glint in the sunlight, but found nothing clearly recognizable as part of one of the plants; and with a frown behind the face plate of his helmet he turned and headed rapidly for the ladder.

On the main deck, six of the ten members of the expedition were waiting when he arrived. Most of them were unconcerned, enjoying one of the rare periods of relaxation—Tick Wesley had not been exaggerating about the constant occupation of the group. The missing three were a pair of petrologists who were "chasing" the shadow, trying to get measurements of any spalling effect from the quick cooling and heating as it passed, and the stratigrapher, Milton Ingersoll. Kinchen was watching the hatch, evidently for the doctor's arrival; and the whole group fell silent at the expression on the newcomer's face.

"What's the matter, Doc? Someone catch cold and put you to work?" Detzel, fuel system expert who doubled as tractor operator while not in flight, put the question. Though only a few of the group had heard the doctor's suspicions about the life discovery, he did not take time to explain in detail, but addressed Kinchen directly.

"The specimens I had out are gone. Someone drove a tractor, over the site."

"Accidentally?"

"I wouldn't know. I'm afraid I didn't mark it." He went to the port overlooking the site of his misfortune, and pointed down to the tracks, clearly visible in the dust. "Does anyone here remember crossing that area— making those particular tracks—in the last twelve hours? Judging by their loneliness, it's only happened once. I should think you'd remember."

THE REST of the group crowded around the port, and one by one denied having driven over that spot. All of them were certain; all were able to describe their work of the last half-day in sufficient detail to show that their memories were trustworthy. As the evidence came in, Imbriano glanced more and more grimly at Kinchen.

"I think Milt will have to do some explaining," he said at last. "He *knew* that I put the stuff there—saw me do it, and talked to me about it. Where is he now?"

"I'd still go easy on demanding explanations, Doc," the leader answered. "Remember, it's his own discovery you're accusing him of destroying, to put it at the very least. What you're really claiming, I don't like even to think. I admit that sort of thing has happened, but I still can't believe that Milt could possibly be so—well, un-balanced, as to try it. Will you please be careful if you must discuss it with him? Or better, let me do it?"

Imbriano frowned. For a moment, he was on the verge of asking whether that was an order, but he was adult enough to realize that the question would not make matters any better.

"All right, Ray," he said.

"Please try to find out, though. This business has wasted enough of our time already." There was a faint chuckle phrase "our time," and the doctor started to whirl around with a hot remark on his lips; but once again he got the better of his emotions, and said nothing. Kinchen tried to fill the awkward gap.

"Why don't you put out a couple of more plates, while Milt's away? He won't know anything about it, and you can find some spot a little farther from the ship where accidents won't happen."

"All right." The doctor stepped across the deck to the table, which was considered his private domain, and then spun to face the others, fury showing plainly on his face.

"Unless someone has a really original sense of humor, there's been another accident," he remarked, keeping his voice under much better control than his features. "The dishes with the lichens are gone. I'll be as objective as I can, to keep our good commander happy, so I'll start by saying—this is far too serious for a joke, practical or otherwise. Did anyone borrow, or otherwise remove, from my table here, six Petri dishes? Each containing some rather crumbly-looking bits of lichen?" There were no answers for a moment, then a collection of

159

negatives. Imbriano looked at the commander. "How about it?"

KINCHEN was extremely uncomfortable. He had been uncomfortable ever since the doctor had first hinted at the possibility of a Piltdown on Ingersoll's part. There was no point in delaying the issue by asking questions about opportunity; Ingersoll had served his turn on watch, alone in the ship, for more than an hour since the dishes had been set out. He *could* have done it. Why he *should* have was not quite so obvious. The astronomer thought for a moment, wishing as he did so that he been able to come as an astronomer rather than a leader of men, which he had never pretended to be. He finally began asking questions.

"How many of you heard directly from Milt of his discovery of plant life?" was his first question. The doctor started to say something, but closed his mouth again. Kinchen glanced at him. "I'm not changing the subject, or postponing the issue, Doc," he added quietly. "How many, please?" Four hands went up.

"How about you, Al? Did you hear about it at all?" Kinchen asked the only one who had not responded— the doctor had made no move, but the answer was already known in his case.

"Bill told me," Detzel answered. "I was asleep when Milt came in. I had the impression he was telling everyone, and had just missed me by chance." The commander nodded.

"So we all knew it," he said slowly. "Then Milton knew about Doc's test since Doc carefully told him. And he knew, furthermore, that the test would show up any Terrestrial organisms. If he were actually trying to pull a Piltdown, what would he do?"

"Destroy the evidence, first of all," answered the doctor promptly. Kinchen looked at him thoughtfully.

"What good would that do?" he asked. "We all knew of the discovery. If we knew it was faked, then…"

"But, in a way, we don't know—or, at least, you refuse to admit that it's proved. And you're right, of course. With the specimens gone, there's no proof. We could never even make the charge."

"IF THAT were all, I'd be quite relieved," Kinchen replied. "However, if he had really done this, and then destroyed the specimens, the fact would be bound to come out among us almost immediately. Either he'd make no more mention of the discovery, which would be a confession in itself, or…"

"Or he'd be as surprised and disappointed as anyone at the disappearance of the specimens, and insist that some enemy had done it to ruin his reputation. And how would we prove differently?" cut in Imbriano. Several pairs of eyes met as their owners considered this aspect of the matter.

The commander was silent for some moments. "I must admit I hope that's what happens," he said at length.

"Why, for goodness sake?" snapped the doctor.

"Because then I will simply send two or three pairs of searchers to the area where he claims to have made the find, and really cover it. If we find more similar specimens, well and good. Milt's charge will have some stuffing—but personally I'd be inclined to keep the matter quiet. If we don't, then we just keep quiet about the whole thing, and Milt is deprived of discovery rights. He can submit his report, but he'll be taking his chances on belief, of course. What's happened to the specimens is certainly unbelievable. That would get the whole thing out of my hands, where I'd much prefer it to be. If, on the other hand, he's sufficiently unbalanced to feel that he's given himself away completely to us—this is now assuming that he's really guilty—I see two courses of action open to him."

"And those are?"

"To kill himself, literally or figuratively—that is, actually destroy himself, or go back to Earth with no reputation, which I for one would find trouble doing—or kill us." The last phrase came so abruptly that no one grasped it completely for several seconds. Then there was a babble of voices.

"He couldn't" was the consensus which made itself most clearly heard after the first few seconds. With that comforting thought, the noise died down; but Kinchen shook his head slowly.

"YOU'RE wrong. He could. Anyone of us could. Have you really failed to grasp how completely each of us has been depending on the others for his life? Each of us has been alone in the ship time and again. Each of us has been in complete charge of food, drink, air, and the transportation back to Earth. You know as well as I that one man could fly this bucket home. Take-off orders are already in the tape, the only variables of noticeable magnitude are due to libration, and those are small enough to be handled by remote control from the computers on Earth—as they were planned to be handled. Your need for me ended when we touched down here. This machine could be started for home at any minute, by any man, and make it."

This point was digested in an even deadlier silence. This time no one looked at anybody else.

"I think that's one possibility we'd better dispose of right now." The quiet voice, which broke the silence, was that of Tick Wesley. "There are three obvious means of getting rid of us, granting that he wanted to. The food, the drink, and the air. Let's check them. Doc, you'd better find whether any of your drugs are missing."

"That won't take long," Imbriano answered. "Just a moment. You might as well hold off on the other checks. If there's nothing missing, there's not much he can have done to food or drink."

The check of his medical supplies took a scant five minutes, and was encouraging. "All accounted for," he said at last. "Better check the air plant, though I don't see what he could do about that without involving himself in the result."

DETZEL and Wesley examined the intricate little pump-and-tank assembly—more intricate than seemed necessary at first, since it had to bubble air into water and get it out again in free fall as well as with weight to keep the liquid separate—but could find nothing. The lights were sound, the circuitry intact, the algae healthy. They returned with this news to the others.

"Then as far as we know, Milt is sincere," Kinchen said with visible relief. "And I can't believe he'd be idiotic enough to leave without taking care of us in some way, after what Doc told him…" Several of the others were shaking their heads, and he remembered. "That's right. There's still the path of straight denial open to him. But that's all right—it's the one I'd like best to have him take. Frankly, I'll be happy as long as there's reasonable chance of his innocence, no matter what unpleasant possibility that will imply about someone else. Let's forget this for the moment and eat. The shadow will be past in a few hours—we're pretty close to it's tip—and there's a lot of work to be done."

"Ben and Hans are coming in with their tractor," someone called from one of the ports. "Better get food ready for them, too. They'll be hungry."

"All right." Frake, whose turn it was to get the meal, disappeared toward the galley, several decks below the air lock level.

"I still would like to know where Milt is and what he's doing," remarked Imbriano. "I thought it was customary to check with someone—no matter who— before going out, in the interest of safety."

Kinchen shrugged. "He didn't, but he's gone. That is, unless a gremlin made off with one of the tractors. He didn't tell us on the other trip, either, remember. I nearly had heart failure when he didn't turn up for fifty hours and I didn't have the slightest notion which way to search, I suppose he'll be back with another discovery." The doctor glanced at him, but made no comment on this closing speech. Perhaps he might have, but he had no chance.

A VOICE came echoing up from the lower levels.

"Commander! Doc! Everyone! Come here!" The voice was that of Frake, and there was quite a jam at the hatch before the six men who rushed for it got themselves sorted out. Imbriano was first out of the tangle, Kinchen last. By the time the commander reached the galley deck, everyone else was staring at what Frake had to show. This, as it turned out, was practically nothing—a fact of some interest, since it should have been their food supply.

"We're—we're cleaned out," Frake said. "There isn't a day's grub left, for the lot of us. How, and where, did it go?"

"Search the ship!" was Kinchen's instant order.

"That will be a waste of time," predicted the doctor. "He could have moved it out with no trouble at all. Instrument and data containers have been going in and out the air lock in a steady stream, practically all the time. None of us would notice the details of anyone else's gear, any more than we notice in particular when someone takes off with a tractor to do his part of the job. We've been too busy to pay attention to other people." There was no humor at the "we" this time.

"Make the search, anyway," the commander repeated. "Everyone but Doc, and Al." The others scattered, their faces serious: the two who remained with the astronomer were even grimmer.

"What is it, sir?" asked the engineer, when they were alone. "You wanted me for some special reason."

"Yes, Al. Taking our food was pointless, unless something else was done, too. Remember we could get to Earth in a hundred hours. Check the power plant— every cubic centimeter of it that's not too hot to be touched. I'll bet you find something before the rest do," he added rather grimly. Detzel nodded, and disappeared downward, Kinchen turned to Imbriano, and eyed him thoughtfully.

"As you say, Doc, I'm a hard man to convince—or didn't you quite get around to saying it? No matter. You seem to be right. Now we'll have to figure out where he is, catch him…"

"Why catch him?"

"I'm sure it will turn out he's taken some essential part of our flight equipment with him, to prevent our simply heading back for Earth and leaving him behind. I'll admit he may be unbalanced, but I still can't picture him as a moron. Wait and see—there's not too much point chasing him until we know what we're looking for."

CHAPTER THREE

VERY LITTLE happened in the next hour. The two men who had been seen approaching came in, and were told of the state of affairs. They had nothing to contribute; they had seen neither Ingersoll nor the missing tractor. No trace was found of the missing food.

Neither of these facts surprised the commander in the least. One, which did, however, was Detzel's failure to find anything whatever wrong with the reactor or any of its auxiliary gear. So far as he could tell, they could have strapped in and left the moon on ten minutes' notice. Kinchen was slightly tempted to do it, but his eternal uncertainty kept him from acting. He thought for a while, then ordered the group to make a check on which trailers, and what kinds, had gone with the tractor presumably containing Ingersoll.

This was accomplished quickly enough, and the conclusion reached that the fellow must have made off with what amounted to a freight train. Four of the heavy-duty trailers had disappeared, in addition to the extra "fuel" carrier. It was easy to see where the food must have gone. It was less easy to see what, other than abandoning the man on the moon, was to be done about it. The group gathered around Kinchen, hoping he'd come up with a decision but quite willing to express ideas of their own if asked. The commander did his own deciding, this time.

"We give twenty-four hours to a search for Milt, with the object of bringing him back if at all possible. We have just one tractor for the purpose. Those who don't go on the search will wind up their various jobs as well as they can without long distance transportation. Volunteers for the search?"

"I'll go!" Imbriano said emphatically. "I'll probably be needed, anyway."

"Maybe—though I hadn't heard you were a psychiatrist. You're probably right about going, though. Let's see..." he glanced over the raised hands. "Al and Bill, you go with Dr. Imbriano. Do your best to catch Milt without hurting him. It seems important to me that we find out whether this has been caused by something about the moon, whether or not you care about Milt himself, try not to get yourselves hurt, and for Pete's sake don't get both tractors crippled a hundred miles from here. There must be a limit to how far a man can walk in a space suit, even on the moon, but I'd rather not collect data on just what it is right now. Al, before you go, could you turn up the heat a trifle? This ship is getting positively chilly."

"It's been that way for some time," Frake remarked, "but I didn't like to say anything."

"What do you expect, in the shadow of a mountain on the moon?" Imbriano asked, with a slight trace of superiority in his tone.

"I'd expect to be cold," Frake said calmly, "but your crack seems irrelevant. We've been in shadow only about ten minutes and I've been cold longer than that. Maybe it was psychological."

"Save it!" snapped Kinchen. "Al, run up the main thermostat as I asked. Then get suited up with Doc and Bill and get going."

TWENTY minutes later, the tractor was rolling. There were two clues to follow; occasional tracks in the dust, and the likelihood that Ingersoll would take his former course, which he had mapped and reported—truthfully, they hoped.

For some time, at least, the two sources of evidence agreed. It seemed likely that the fugitive would be forced to travel quite slowly, since he was carrying a long train of trailers. These would not only be a heavy load for his turbine, but might also prove a maneuvering problem if he got into any tight spots. If this proved not to be true, catching the fellow would probably be impossible; he had quite evidently taken an extra supply of turbine juice, using for the purpose the only spare carrier adapted for the stuff. If the pursuers did not sight him before reaching their range limit, they were out of luck.

Sighting the other vehicle was also likely to be a problem. In full sunlight, of course, the metal would glint and be recognizable over vast distances; but in shadows, where the only illumination was reflected light from the surrounding peaks, the problem was different. They carried a snooper—an infra-red viewer intended to help map the crater in terms of equilibrium—temperature variations as a clue to dust depth and petrological differences, but its field was narrow. Detzel used it on every deep shadow they passed, while Frake drove and Imbriano used his eyes; but no sign of the other tractor appeared, except occasional tread marks.

THEY WERE heading south and a trifle east (not the selenographer's east, but *left* of south) toward a spot where a small crater breaks Moretus' southern rim. Here, according to Ingersoll's report, he had found a pass out of the walled plain, which was possible for the tractors. The pursuers reached the area in a reasonable time, and found no difficulty in tracing the path, though there was no way of being sure whether the tracks had been left on the original trip or only a few hours before. The driving was hard on the nerves; grades were steep along the way, and steeper to either side. They eventually reached the top, skirted the five-mile crater, made a last radio check with the ship, and were about to break line-of-sight contact with their friends when Kinchen suddenly interrupted Wesley's routine acknowledgement of their call.

"Al!" his voice came through clearly, with no attempt to cover its owner's anxiety. "We've found what was done to the ship. You may have to come back—listen. The upper manual safeties on the main tank were both opened—we can't tell exactly when—and left that way. We don't know how much water we lost from evaporation, and we can't get the valves closed. Any ideas?"

Detzel snatched the microphone from the doctor, who had been handling communications.

"The tanks were completely full; at least initially. We never touched them on landing. With those valves wide, the water would have boiled—we should have felt the vibration at that point if we were in the ship. It must have been happening while Ingersoll was on watch. Boiling water would spatter into the vents, and perhaps outside them, and as the evaporation pulled heat from it it would freeze. The valves are probably jammed with ice.

"You may not have lost all that much from the tanks, since a layer of ice would have formed sooner or later on the surface and cut down the evaporation rate. That must be what made the ship so cold—evaporation into a vacuum. I should think you could free the valves by simply melting the ice—you may have to do some improvising with electric heaters, but it shouldn't be difficult. When you get the valves shut, keep the main thermostat up the way I left it. When the ship temperature really starts to climb, the ice inside the tanks will have melted and then you can reset it to make the place comfortable. With liquid in the tanks, you can compute the amount of juice from the reading of any of the static pressure gauges—preferably Number One, the lowest. There's a table in my kit for turning pressure readings into quantity for that tank under various acceleration conditions. We'd better go on, it seems to me. Whether or not there's enough juice left to get us home doesn't make much difference in what we can do about it."

Imbriano interrupted. "Why go on, though? Ingersoll must have been raving mad to pull that trick. It would doom him as surely as it does us, if too much water really boiled from the tank. He's probably driven himself over a cliff or opened his cab with his helmet off by this time, anyway!"

NO ONE IN the cab really heard Kinchen's answer to this. It came through, but it came through mixed with another voice. It was a dry, clear voice, enunciated so perfectly that the words were plain even mixed with those of Kinchen, and clear enough to permit the mocking overtones to be grasped. All three listeners got every word of it; none of them could remember afterward what Kinchen had been saying at the same moment.

"That sounds like our good doctor!" the mocking voice came. "The doctor who knows so much. The doctor who shouldn't really have come to the moon at all, since he knows so much about it—knows it hasn't any life, and knows it hasn't any water. Such a smart fellow! And he feels sure I've killed myself, so that I won't have to starve on the moon like the others, because of course that dope Ingersoll could never find anything on the moon to replace water lost from the tanks! Oh, no!

"Tell me, Dr. Imbriano, how do you manage to live with your own brilliance? Doesn't it overwhelm you at times? Of course, you're right about one thing—you ought to go back. You won't get to water with the fuel you have. I can wait, wait until you're gone, and fuel up my tractor and come back, and refill the ship's tank, too. And I can take off for Earth with a very sick group of friends, and they just might die en route, and be jettisoned in space, so no one could ever tell just what they died of. And maybe they were a little crazy, because they destroyed my life specimens—don't you think that's a reasonable chain of events, you self-righteous, pompous, know-it-all? Don't you?" Ingersoll's voice fell silent, and the men in the cab looked at each other.

"He's really gone," muttered Detzel. "Plant life—which I could and did swallow—but now water, which I certainly can't."

His attention was attracted by Kinchen's voice, asking why the tractor had stopped broadcasting. Evidently Ingersoll's waves were not reaching the ship, which was hardly surprising. Detzel extended the microphone to the doctor, so that he could explain what had happened, but Imbriano shook his head impatiently. He was obviously bothered by something, and didn't want his thought interrupted, so Detzel himself explained to the commander. Kinchen listened silently.

"If he's really out of range, you might as well come back," he said when the engineer had finished. "I wish those fellows who gave us all the tests before takeoff had been able to pick that up. We've lost one man, may lose nine more, and the project itself can't possibly be completed now. All that's over and above the fact that I liked Ingersoll."

DETZEL was about to acknowledge the order when the doctor held up a hand imperiously.

"Wait!" he exclaimed. "Can he possibly be out of range of the tractor yet, if we can hear him on the radio?"

"It's hard to be sure, without knowing how far from a straight line the ground will force us to go, but I'd say it was unlikely. Why?"

"Because we'll have to get him—*have* to. He's not crazy the way you think. I'm no psychologist, I admit, but I think I know what's wrong, and it's my fault. Sure, he's a bit paranoid—but I rode him too hard. If there's anything that pushed him over the edge into this nonsense, it was the way I treated him—you could read that, in the way he was talking just now. I'm the one he's down on, and—well, let's not go into it. We've got to get him."

"I can't see it," retorted Frake. "What difference does the cause make? Even if you feel guilty, and want to rescue him, what difference does it make if he's killed us all? I don't blame you, but..."

"That's not it—at least, not all of it. Sure, I feel pretty rotten about what I've done to Milt, but that's not the whole story. He's not raving mad. He wants revenge on me. *How can he get it unless he's telling the truth about the water?*"

THERE was a moment of silence; then Detzel spoke.

"Either you're speaking from knowledge that's way outside my field, or you're filling in a graph with a lot of guesswork, or you're nuttier than Ingersoll," he remarked. "Just how do you get the notion of water on the moon? Every part of that blasted rock ball gets well above the boiling point of water, or even what the boiling point would be at sea level on Earth. And the moon is not able to hold any gas that has a molecular weight of less than about sixty. Hydrate minerals like gypsum form from the evaporation of salt solutions, and if the moon ever—at any time in the distant past—had

174

any lakes or seas I'll drink an equivalent quantity as soon as it's proved."

"Never mind the cosmology," snapped Imbriano. "It's irrelevant. Ingersoll, remember, is a geologist. I don't think he's a very good one, and it's my own fault that I didn't keep that to myself. But he's not a complete dope and I never said he was. He claims, indirectly, that he's found water. He should be competent to know whether he has or not. If you don't want to stay on the moon to be discovered by the next expedition, then get back to the controls and start us along that trail once more. Ingersoll may be really crazy, but I'm betting he isn't. Give me the mike."

The engineer obeyed, muttering something about "wishful thinking," and started up the turbine. Imbriano called the commander.

"We're not coming back just yet," he said. "I can't explain why over the radio. Expect us when you hear from us." He snapped the microphone onto its hook with a gesture of finality, and settled back into his seat with an expression on his face that prevented either of the others from speaking. The tractor nosed its way along the small crater rim and began to switchback down into the incredibly broken country between Moretus and Short. The trail was clear enough, here; most of the ground was not only too rough for a tractor but too steep for dust, and everywhere a vehicle could go there was enough dust to take its tracks. More than once the marks showed multiple; evidently Ingersoll was retracing his earlier path.

FOR SOME fifteen miles projectile distance, which the torturous way made into more like forty, they followed westward between Moretus and Short. Then the trail led up the outer slopes of a ten-mile crater, which overlapped the northern rim of Short, and down a terrifying ridge where the two merged out onto the somewhat smoother floor of the latter. The trail was more difficult to see here, but the drivers were catching on to the logic Ingersoll seemed to have used in finding the passes; and between this and the occasional tracks, they were able to follow almost straight across the thirty-mile walled plain of Short to another intruding pit on its southern rim. They sloped up along the latter, and eventually emerged on the eastern brink of Newton. They were perhaps ninety miles from the ship in a straight line, but had ridden considerably more than twice that distance.

The scene below them was something that the Earth could not offer, and even the moon would have had trouble in equaling. Newton comes the closest of any ringed plain of its size to having the entire floor visible from one of the walls. Usually the far side is well below the horizon; but Newton is *deep*. The men were not at the highest point of the rim; that was nearby, a four-and-a-half-mile peak more impressive than any mountain of Earth, since the four and a half miles was above the nearby plain rather than a sea several hundred miles away. Even from the point where the tractor was parked, the drop to the central plain was stomach-wrenching—something better than twice the depth of Arizona's Grand Canyon.

A little ahead of them, the wall curved in and descended toward, even beyond, the center of the ring, almost as though Newton were two partly fused craters. It seemed likely that the trail they were following would go down this way; the fugitive had certainly come this way before, and it seemed unlikely that he would have resisted the temptation to make the descent along what looked like a God-given path.

NORTH and south the walls curved westward, finally swinging back together and meeting some seventy miles away. Inside, they alternated stretches of appalling steepness with what amounted to broad terraces; on the far side, the lowest of these could just barely be seen above the bulge of the moon's curvature. The curve itself, showed plainly on the floor of Newton, though even allowing for this the "plain" was far from level. The northern half seemed deeper than the southern, carrying on to some extent the impression of two merged craters; much of the deeper floor was invisible in the shadow of the north rim, the sun being less than fifteen degrees above the northern "horizon." It was less than a day past local noon.

"You know I think this is a pretty bad place to park if we don't want Milt to know we're coming," remarked Detzel after absorbing the scenery for some minutes. "This metal buggy must be gleaming all over the crater. If he's anywhere inside, he must know we're here already."

Imbriano didn't answer directly. He was scanning every dark patch he could see within Newton's ring with the infra-red viewer, and the northern part of the floor was a lot to cover with the narrow-field instrument. "I should think that even a man in a space suit would radiate visibly against that background," he muttered. "It's cold. Not a flicker on the screen, at any gain this thing can take. Any metal reflection in the sunlight areas?"

"Nothing so far." Both the other men spoke together.

Frake added, "You want a spell on that snooper?"

"All right." Imbriano removed his face from the visor, and handed the gear forward. For some time there was little sound as Frake very slowly and methodically scanned the impenetrable darkness below. Then he stopped, and played with the gain control for a moment or two.

"That should be it," he said. "It's about the right temperature for a condenser radiator. I can't see any motion, but he's a long way off—forty miles, I'd guess, though it's hard to be sure when we can't see the bottom contour. He could be on a hill a lot closer."

"Where?" both the others asked simultaneously.

"SEE THAT peak just coming up into sunlight on the floor, just below another on the far rim? There. It's warm enough to show on the screen. Now, swing the viewer to the right slowly—just a couple of degrees— that's it; you should have him."

"There's a spot on the screen, all right," Imbriano admitted. "I can't read these colors well enough to judge temperature, but you should know this gadget better than I. If you say it's the right temperature, it must be

Milt. I can't imagine any other source of warmth down there. Let's go."

"Which way?"

"Keep along the trail. I know it takes us farther away from that radiation source, but I can't see diving straight down hill toward it."

Detzel nodded, started the turbine again, and sent the vehicle crawling forward. As they had expected, the trail led out onto the spur, which merged, into the floor miles across the plain. It was impossible to follow rapidly; on the original trip, Ingersoll must have been amazingly lucky to find the way down in the time he had been away. It turned out that the trail reached the floor well before the buttress did, switching down the north side so they were able to keep the radiation source in sight nearly to the bottom. On the floor itself, of course, the curve of the moon put the other machine below the horizon.

The trail now led almost straight toward the northern shadows; the sun crawled visibly toward the scarp miles above as they advanced.

"We're going to need lights here," remarked Frake. "There's reflection from the peaks, all right, but I wouldn't trust it to keep us out of a crack."

Detzel grunted agreement; Imbriano was silent. A faint memory was crawling up into his consciousness. He kept sweeping the darkness ahead of them, hoping the other tractor would show on the screen; but the minutes crawled by with nothing appearing.

THE SUN vanished at last. The ground about them could just be seen in the light reflected from the ring of peaks, but as Frake had predicted, the lights of the tractor were needed. If the other vehicle were still in shadow, it must be using lights too; but of course these would be almost impossible to see unless pointed straight at the pursuers. Imbriano kept the viewer in use.

The ground, when they first entered the shadow, was the typical, dark, dusty lunar plain. At first, they saw an occasional track; then they must have wandered a little off the line, for no more of these appeared. When Detzel finally pointed this out, and asked the doctor which way to go. Imbriano answered, "As you are. Keep angling west, and toward the north rim. That's about the direction to the spot where he was, and there's something else I want to see, anyway."

"You won't see much with these lights," replied the driver. "You'd better wait until the sun gets here. It looks as though we might be waiting, anyway; turbine juice is running low. We're about to the halfway mark on the gauge, and there's a big hill to climb the way back." Imbriano smiled, seemed about to speak, but didn't.

Then, slowly, the ground changed. Its color under the lights was paler, as though more feldspar were showing in the predominantly basaltic rock, and the doctor began to nod slowly. At last the surface seemed almost white.

"Bear a little to the left—five degrees or so," he said abruptly. Detzel obeyed without asking why, and silence fell again for another ten minutes. Then something appeared on the ground ahead.

"Tracks!" exclaimed Frake, the first to see them. "We've found the trail again!"

"I thought we'd be pretty sure to cross it," Imbriano said quietly, "and of course, it would show up well here."

"Why of course? Because the dust is so light-colored? I'm surprised it's deep enough, on this flat surface. The trail looks almost like marks in snow."

"Uh-huh." Imbriano drawled the answer in a manner, which would not have been tolerated even in a child actor, but the tone got his hearers' attention. They whirled in their seats to face him.

"Are you implying it really is snow?" gasped Detzel.

"EYES FRONT, driver. I am too much of an ignoramus to dare imply anything. I think 1 owe Milt Ingersoll a profound apology, though. If one of you will switch on the radio, I'll try to make it. He might be close enough for diffraction to get him even if he isn't quite line-of-sight from here."

"Wait a minute." Detzel made no move toward the radio. "I don't care what the stuff out there *looks* like. If it has a boiling point much below that of feldspar, I'll melt and drink it. You know as well as I that even ice has a respectable vapor pressure near its freezing point, and when the sun gets on this stuff it's a darned sight hotter than the freezing point of ice."

"Minor catch, Al. *When does the sun get on it?*"

"Why—in the daytime, of course. It…"

"I hate to be a party pooper, but isn't it daytime right now, on this part of the moon? Correct me if I'm wrong."

Detzel whistled gently. "You're right. Some of this shadow would get light when the sun was farther east or west, but most of it, right against the wall particularly—but wait. What about seasonal changes?"

"On the moon? With its axis about one degree from the perpendicular to its *heliocentric* orbit? Sorry. I don't know how permanent that axial orientation is—with all the perturbations there must be—but I'll bet it hasn't wandered very far from its present line since the moon's rotation matched its geocentric revolution. Some of this area may have been dark for only a few thousand or a few million years, but right in against the cliffs it's been more like two or three billion, I expect."

"I see what Milt didn't like about you. You're too darned right. All right, I concede, I'll drink the stuff. But wait a minute. Granting that it could stay here, how did it *get* here? I don't buy rain, springs, frost, dew, rivers, or any other normal way."

"You'd better not drink it. I expect it's ice only by courtesy. I wouldn't be surprise if a good healthy lacing of ammonia and perhaps methane were there as well as water. As far as how goes, I don't really know. But as a working guess, the moon must have passed through quite a few comet tails in the last couple of billion years."

"But comet tails are thin—a ton to the million miles of length, or something like that…"

"Two billion years is a long time. But I don't insist on that. I haven't tried to work it out quantitatively, and wouldn't be able to get an answer if I did try. Maybe the solar system went through a nebula or something—I don't know. I just say there's something like snow out there, and Ingersoll seems to have convinced himself that's what it is, judging by his remarks a few hours ago. That's why I say—give me the radio. I want to apologize to him." Detzel obeyed in dazed silence, and Imbriano sent a call pulsing out over the crater floor, but there was no answer. He stopped after a few minutes, judging that he either wasn't being heard or was being snubbed, and they kept on along the trail.

CHAPTER FOUR

PERHAPS an hour later, after several more unanswered calls, they reached a spot where something seemed to have happened. There was a dark patch of irregular shape on the "snow." The white deposit was now some half an inch deep on the plain; but here it seemed to have been cleared away. The edges of the bare region were sharp and well defined, though irregular. The men all reached the same conclusion at the same tine; they had all shoveled too many snowy driveways to be fooled here.

"He scraped the stuff up to put in his tank!" exclaimed Frake. "That's what he meant about water, all right—though he'll spend a good long time getting up enough to make much impression on the ship's tank, I should think. But hadn't we better do the same? Our own fluid gauge is reading lower than I really like, at this distance from Moretus."

"How about it, Al?" asked Imbriano. "Suppose this stuff is largely ammonia and/or methane? What would happen if we used it in the tractor?"

"Either one is all right so far as straight theory goes," Detzel replied carefully. "They're both low-boiling, low molecular weight compounds, which would operate perfectly well in a turbine. I'm just afraid they might be a little too low boiling. That would cut down efficiency, and at our working temperature their vapor pressures might be too much for our tank."

"I was afraid of that. Is there any way we can make sure, safely?"

"I should think so. There are safety valves on the tanks—after all, even water is apt to get pretty hot if the tractor stands in the sun for long. The regular relief valves *might* keep things safe, but I could ease off their springs a bit to make them safer. If we don't put too much of the stuff in at once, we might get away with it. After all, Ingersoll seems to have."

"HE SEEMS to have loaded the stuff. We *don't* know that he got away with it," responded the doctor dryly. "I suggest, Al, that we quietly put one pinch of the stuff in the tank and see what happens—in fact, could we draw a bucket or can or something of water from the tank and put our pinch of snow in that, at some distance from the tractor? I admit I'd be happier that way."

"I guess a cup of water would last long enough for that. We'll try, anyway." The three men donned their helmets, pumped a reasonable fraction of the cab's air into the low-pressure economy tank, and opened up. Detzel found a paper-drinking cup and stepped out, making his way around to the trailer, which carried the fluid tank. There he bent, held the cup under a stopcock, and quickly opened and closed the latter. Water squirted out violently; it was warm enough to have a vapor pressure of several centimeters of mercury. The stream of liquid hit the cup and splashed, but enough remained inside to be useful. Detzel grimaced behind his face plate.

"Offends my economical soul," he remarked, staring at the bubbling, frothing liquid.

"You'll be wasting more if you don't get moving," retorted Frake. "Get some of that snow in before everything boils away."

Detzel obeyed. He took a small scraper from its place on the side of the trailer and walked over to the edge of the clear area. He set the cup on the ground where the men could see it; Frake was holding the beam of a flashlight on the scene. He picked up a bit of the snowy material on the end of the scraper, and tipped it into the cup.

The results were spectacular; as Imbriano said a moment later, "Water holds quite a bit of latent heat, doesn't it?" The contents of the cup fountained skyward and failed to return, fading into invisible vapor before the moon's feeble gravity could do much about it. The cup itself was intact, but the fact was rather surprising to the witnesses.

"I don't think any valves made will take that, or let the tank take it," Detzel remarked. "I'm afraid we'll have to depend on what's still in the tank to get us back to the ship."

"WHAT?" Even Imbriano was startled to hear the dry voice of Ingersoll in his headset once more. "What? Can't the brilliant doctor solve such a simple problem? Even when he just mentioned the answer? But of course, you have a slight disadvantage. You have only one fuel tank, haven't you? I very carelessly brought the spare with me. It was empty when I filled it with snow, friends—no water. No stored heat to speak of. I've packed the snow into it, and we'll just let it melt very slowly, and the methane can evaporate quietly through the valves, and the ammonia stay in solution if it wants...

"I'll tell you what, good doctor; why don't you just dump all your water out of that tank? Then in a little while it will be cool enough to take the snow safely, and you can go back to starve with your friends—for you can't catch me, can you? I have *two* tanks, and that makes the big difference, doesn't it? I'm going, by the way, and I'm sure you can see me with your instruments, but you can't follow. You don't dare go any way but back to Moretus, do you? Of course, I'm not going far either—I'm not going to take this tank out into sunlight for a while—but you don't dare even chase me around in circles, do you? Fuel is getting a little short."

He broke off as abruptly as he had started. The drivers looked at the doctor. He shrugged invisibly in his suit, and led the way back inside the cab. There, with air once more about them and their helmets off, Frake finally spoke up.

"Well? Was he right?" He was looking at Imbriano as he spoke.

"I'm not the engineer," the doctor said wearily. "So far as I can see, he is perfectly right. Personally, I'm optimistic about the fuel in the ship's tanks. I don't think we could possibly have lost much before the ice layer formed. But that doesn't make me any happier about Ingersoll."

"Maybe we'd better tell him about the ice stopping the evaporation," suggested Frake.

"You do it. He certainly wouldn't believe me," the doctor replied wearily. Frake took the microphone.

HE CALLED Ingersoll's name several times, without answer; then he told about the freezing in the tank, sure that the other was listening. He ended with an air of frankness.

"I admit we don't know there's enough to get us home," he said, "but you know I'm talking sense when I say there's a good chance of it. If you want to take that chance, just stay where you are and watch. You can probably see the takeoff from here. You'll know about when it will be—you can guess how long it will take us to get back. We're starting now. You can stay or come, as you please."

He hung up the microphone, and Detzel started the tractor out toward the sunlight, slanting back toward the foot of the trail leading down from the rim. Imbriano rode with his head turned over his right shoulder, in the general direction that he believed the other vehicle to be. There was no sound from the radio.

But it was Detzel who first saw the other machine, and called their attention to it. It was paralleling their course, half a mile to the north, and gradually pulling ahead of them. It was just barely visible; almost all that could be seen was scattered light from its lenses, and the streak of illumination stretching over the ground ahead of it. Detzel took the microphone

"Glad you're coming, Milt," he called. "Want to lead? You must know this road a lot better than we do, so you can go faster safely." There was a brief pause.

"All right. Pull over this way, and fall in behind me." The voice had lost all trace of emotion. Detzel slanted obediently to the left, and relaxed a trifle—he had been giving close thought to the problem of navigation. Imbriano did not; and it was just as well.

THEY WERE a scant hundred yards from the other machine, and were just about able to make it out in the light reflected from the mountains, when Detzel's attention was jerked back to full operations level. With a turn that threatened to snap the couplings of its trailers, Ingersoll's tractor was whipping around; its lights glared directly into their eyes, and Imbriano and Frake ducked instinctively. Fortunately, Detzel's reactions were of a more constructive nature; he wrenched their own vehicle to the right, and managed to avoid the first charge.

"Get your helmets on!" he snapped to the others. "Then take the wheel, Bill, while I do mine. If he even grazes us there'll be no air in this cab."

"We can outrun him. He's pulling a bigger load," the doctor pointed out as he fitted his helmet in place.

"We could on the straight—but we're not sure we can go straight. If anyone knows the crevasses around here, it's Ingersoll, not me."

"Even he shouldn't know them too well. He can't have spent all his time exploring cracks," Frake put in optimistically.

"He doesn't have to know them at all to have a big advantage," snapped Detzel. "The sad fact is that we're going first. If we can keep going, he can. We can keep ahead just as long as I don't have to detour."

"Head out into the sunlight!" cried Imbriano. "He won't dare take that trailer of snow out there. It would boil too fast."

"We don't know what he'd dare. It's a metal tank, and would take a while to heat up. And if he's willing to risk his own life in a collision, he can't be very rational anyway. I'm already on the way toward sunlight, in case you hadn't noticed."

"Put on more juice! He's catching up!" called Frake. Detzel tried, but the turbine was already whirling at its safe limit.

"Something's wrong. Our trailer must be dragging," he snapped. "We didn't take time to service it properly before we set out on this junket."

"That's not it. I can see now. The back right tire is flat. Either it picked a gruesome time to hit something sharp, or Milt nicked it on that first pass."

"IF WE CAN'T outrun him, we'll have to outmaneuver him," grunted Detzel. "We should still be able to make tighter turns than he can, tire or no tire. Tell me when he's about twenty yards back."

"He's closer than that already, I'd say, though it's hard to be sure with the lights right in my eyes." Detzel's answer was another twist to the right. At the same moment, Imbriano started the economy pump, since they all had their helmets sealed by this time. Neither of the others noticed; Detzel would probably have objected to the waste of power if he had.

The turn was almost, but not quite, successful. The other machine grazed the rear of the trailer, some projection on it ripping their other back tire. Fortunately, the fuel tank in front made the trailer's center of gravity a trifle ahead of the middle pair of wheels, so it didn't settle too badly on the back ones except under acceleration; but the additional flatting of the middle tires added quite a bit of drag.

For a moment, it looked as though Detzel might be overcoming this disadvantage. He held his turn, and the other train was unable to match it, as he had hoped. Slowly he drew ahead; then he was parallel, going the other way; then drawing up behind as he lapped Ingersoll. Then they were travelling only a yard or two away from the back trailer of the other machine, and matching its angular speed. As they reached this point, Imbriano opened the door by his seat and swung out.

For a moment, neither of the others noticed. By the time they did, he was climbing across the back of the cab and almost within reach of Ingersoll's rear trailer. He reached, but couldn't quite make it.

"Closer, Al," he snapped. The others heard his voice, didn't for a moment realize where he was since the suit radios gave little indication of distance, and Detzel obeyed without asking why. Then Frake looked back, discovered the doctor missing, and after a moment located him.

"Doc! You idiot!" he cried. The call distracted Detzel, but fortunately not enough to disturb his driving. "What's the matter?" he asked without taking his eyes from the other vehicle.

"Doc's climbing onto Milt's trailer! He's nuts!"

"SHUT UP, stupid!" Imbriano's voice came. "Well, never mind. It's too late now." Frake had forgotten that they were now using the suit radios, and Ingersoll could hear anything they said. The doctor, with secrecy at an end, addressed the geologist directly.

"Here I am, Milt. Right on your rear trailer. Any ideas about how to run into me now? You might as well leave the other tractor alone. Getting it won't get me, will it?"

The answer that came back was unprintable, except for the concluding sentence: "Anyone who helps you needs squashing, too." The larger train swerved away and slowed down, trying to bring Detzel ahead, but the engineer was alert and held his position to the other's right rear.

Imbriano, holding firmly to the body of the trailer, spoke again. "Don't waste too much fuel, Milt. You may find you don't have much to spare, after all." He began to crawl forward along the train as he finished speaking. The bodies of the vehicle were mostly empty—they never knew why Ingersoll had taken so many—and the spare tank containing the snow was bolted to the front of the second one in line. The tank on the first was, of course, actually in service.

Reaching dangerously around the snow tank, Imbriano found the pin of the coupling, which connected the trailer to the one in front, and pulled.

He was unable to move it; there was too much tension on the coupling as long as the tractor was pulling. There were several cases on the front trailer, however—probably the missing food—which prevented Ingersoll from seeing what the doctor was doing; and this uncertainty led the geologist to solve the other's problem for him.

Thinking that Imbriano was damaging his precious reserve tank, Ingersoll began alternately braking and accelerating in an effort to shake him off. This was nearly successful, but it also enabled the doctor to work the pin free after a few cycles, since each time the push changed to a pull or vice versa there was an instant when it was loose. At last he got it out, and had the satisfaction of seeing the tractor and front trailer bound away from him as Ingersoll applied power once more.

THE GEOLOGIST realized instantly what had happened, cut around in as tight a circle as he could to bring his lights on the trailers and Imbriano, and stopped. He evidently wasn't ready to come out; it was too dark to see inside his cab—especially past his lights—but the pause suggested that he was helmeting up and pumping back his air. Imbriano assumed that he was preparing to come out, anyway, and thought of a delaying move.

"Just a minute, Milt—don't come out yet. If I see your cab door open, you'll see this stopcock do the same thing. How about it?" Imbriano had his gloved hand on the bottom tank drain.

For a moment there was silence. Then, "Go ahead and open it. Here I come!"

The doctor couldn't see the cab door open beyond the lights, but he wasn't looking anyway. He carefully opened the stopcock and sprang back, expecting a jet of vapor comparable to the one from the cup not long before. He was watching for it so anxiously that he almost didn't see Ingersoll coming, for the watching job took no longer than he had expected. Nothing happened.

Fortunately for the doctor, Ingersoll had seen the whole thing, and he came to a stop beside the trailer and laughed.

"Smart boy, Doc. I suppose you expected the stuff to boil right out and leave me stranded, didn't you? You didn't remember that the tank has never been in the sun since it was filled, and it had no water in it, and had been out of the sunlight long enough to cool down even before it was filled. Where did you expect the energy to come from? Or doesn't the medical profession believe in conservation of energy? Why, you little..." his language became profane and irrelevant once more, and he made a leap in Imbriano's direction.

The doctor had plenty of time to get out of the way; and his own leap took him out of the direct beams of the headlights, so that for a moment he effectively vanished. Ingersoll started to follow; then a flash of reason crossed his mind, and he headed back for the cab of his own tractor. He got the idea more quickly than any of the others, and made it with plenty of time. He had left the turbine idling, so there was no delay in starting, and neither the doctor nor Frake, who had also leaped from their tractor the moment Detzel brought it to a halt, had a chance to get aboard Ingersoll's.

"Get back with Al!" called Imbriano. "Get back in the tractor, and keep it out of the way. I'm safe enough. Maybe he'll cool down enough to reason with after he's made a few passes at me. Unless he's taught that machine to jump, he'll never catch a man on foot with it!"

Frake agreed, though his words were nearly drowned in another flood of language from Ingersoll. Imbriano was promptly given the opportunity of proving his claim that he could keep out of the way of a tractor.

HIS IMAGINATION supplied the thunderous turbine whine, which the lunar vacuum could not transmit. Some sound, but not much, came through tracks, ground, and feet; but practically, the chase might have been recorded on an old silent film. Frake, later, claimed he was surprised not to see subtitles; but his sense of humor was not very subtle.

Imbriano was not feeling humorous at all. He was able to dodge, all right, but it was not very easy, and he was afraid of leaping too far. A bad landing could be disastrous, since not very much has to go wrong with a space suit to kill its occupant. After a few passes, which would have won very little applause in a Spanish bull-ring but were quite as exciting for Imbriano as he wished, it occurred to him that Ingersoll might be a little slower if the dodging were being done around his precious reserve tank. Accordingly, the doctor made his next leap or two in this direction, and began playing tag around the stranded trailers.

He was still hoping that Ingersoll might cool down and be reasonable; but there was no sign of such an event, and he couldn't think of anything to say that might have a calming effect. Throughout the whole affair, he had been worried by the feeling of guilt he had expressed earlier, and the worry may have slowed him down—certainly some of his escapes were narrower than they needed to be.

Then a different feeling began to take hold of him. However reasonable Ingersoll's original resentment may have been, this grimly-determined effort to repay unpleasantness and discourtesy with murder was going a little too far. Imbriano's sympathy and guilt-feeling began to give way to resentment and anger; his temper, never outstandingly good, was wearing thin. He was thinking, now, in terms of force rather than persuasion.

But that did him little good; granted that a man on foot could keep from being harmed by the man in a tractor, there seemed nothing whatever he could do on the offensive. Certainly Imbriano could think of nothing. He kept as close as he could to the stranded trailer, answered the questions of Detzel and Frake as reassuringly as his breath permitted, and kept moving. He didn't get onto the trailer itself; later he convinced himself, without much trouble, that his own subconscious kept him off.

THE END of the contest was, in one way, something of an anticlimax. Imbriano had thought of nothing brilliant; Frake and Detzel had made no contribution; and Ingersoll had shown no sign of giving up when the whole situation changed—instantly and without warning.

The doctor had suffered his closest shave yet, just barely escaping the charging treads, and had ducked around the front end of the train to its right side. Ingersoll made his closest turn thus far, cutting a trifle left to get his single attached trailer clear and then swinging around so as almost to graze the front of the motionless one. There was no collision; Detzel had his lights on the scene at the moment, and he, Frake, and Imbriano himself were all certain that nothing solid touched the stranded vehicle. Imbriano, who was actually touching it at the time, was sure he would have felt the impact.

Nevertheless, something happened. It was not an explosion—at least not exactly in the conventional sense. The tank, which had been filled with "snow" opened almost deliberately, and sprayed over everything in front of it a furiously boiling, dense, misty vapor, which glowed a bright blue-green, dazzling even against the background of the brilliantly-sunlit mountains. It covered Ingersoll's cab completely; and blinded by the featureless glare, he brought his machine to a stop. That was enough for Detzel, who had been waiting for any sort of opportunity. He hurled his own tractor toward the other, angled it across Ingersoll's front so that the geologist was cramped between Detzel's tractor and the detached trailers. His own trailer, still attached, prevented him from backing without making a "cut," which his front end was not free to do. Ingersoll, or rather his machine, was pinned completely. Getting the man himself, at odds of three to one with the one under a steering wheel, was not too difficult.

"I HOPE they can straighten him out on Earth," Imbriano said soberly to Kinchen a dozen hours later. "He's way beyond me. He had made a real discovery there in Newton—he must have made it on the first trip, to have planned the second as he did. Instead of reporting it, and getting all the credit he seems to have wanted so badly, he pulls this incredibly complex trick. It's like a kid who's daydreamed all the details of a party he's going to attend, and flies into a tantrum when the facts don't follow his imagined program. I think Milt

planned the plant discovery before we ever left Earth—
he must have, to have brought the lichens with him—
and wasn't quick enough on the uptake to throw the
game aside when he made the real discovery. Life
moved too fast for him.

"Of course, it moved too fast for me, too. I still can't
see what happened to his tank, back there. As far as I
can see, he was perfectly right about the snow still being
solid and there not being enough energy to do anything."

"You surprise me," grunted Kinchen.

"Why?" asked the doctor.

"You're admitting that you don't know." Imbriano
flushed, started an angry retort, then calmed down.

"Don't rub it in, Chief. I feel enough of a heel
already. I suppose it was that which helped push Milt as
far as he went. I don't say I'll stop it, because habits are
hard to break, but I'll try. What did happen to the snow,
though?"

"I don't *know*, either," the astronomer replied. "It will
take analysis to make sure. I *think*, though, that your
suggestion about the snow collecting from space—
nebular material, comet's tails, or what have you—is
probably right. But it isn't—or a lot of it isn't—nice
plain water, ammonia, and methane..."

"THERE'S a lot of radiation in space, and a lot of
innocent molecules floating around there get knocked
apart. What you have left is radicals—highly-reactive
fragments of molecules: NH, OH, C2, CH2, and so on.
I suppose equilibrium temperature there in Newton's
permanent shadow can't be more than twenty or thirty
degrees absolute, so the radicals were "frozen"—held

below even their very low activation temperature. I'm a little surprised you were able to run the tractors over the stuff safely—but I suppose the treads were pretty cold by the time you got there.

"As for what finally touched off that tank, my guess would be the exhaust from Milt's safety valves. You say he was, running the machine full blast for several minutes, and even in that environment it wouldn't take what water he had left very long to heat up—after all, it must have been more than half gone by then anyway."

"It was," confirmed Detzel. "We transferred it to our own tank, and didn't manage to fill up even then. Without it, we'd have walked the last fifty miles back here."

"Well, that's my hypothesis, then. I'm pretty happy we don't have to salvage some of that snow for the ship, though I suppose we could probably get away with it— add it a tiny bit at a time, and then let it react. The products would probably be useable enough. They'd be largely the water, ammonia, and methane that Milt thought they were. That cleans up practically everything, I guess."

"Practically?" Imbriano was curious.

Kinchen looked at him narrowly. "Just how sure are you that the plants Ingersoll discovered are Terrestrial, and that he was faking the find?"

Imbriano hesitated before answering.

"I know what I think, but I've done enough damage broadcasting it already," he said at last. "I wish some of those specimens had been saved, and I certainly wish I'd had a chance to see what exposure to moon conditions did to those I put out. If they'd survived, or even formed viable spores…"

"They'd have been quite radical, wouldn't they?" asked Frake.

He wondered why *he* was sent to look for more lichens.

THE END